LUST FOR YOUTH

LUST FOR YOUTH

WARNER JACKSON

CUTTING EDGE

ISBN-13: 978-1-954840-12-6

Also published as *My Mother, The Madam..*

Published by
Cutting Edge Books
PO Box 8212
Calabasas, CA 91372
www.cuttingedgebooks.com

CHAPTER ONE

A T NINE THAT MORNING it had been merely drizzling, but, now at half past eleven, rain fell in heavy torrents. Water gushed along Minnesota avenue in Kansas City, Kansas in front of Smiley's tavern. Along the curbs floated loose newspapers, loose twigs and other litter.

On these kind of rainy mornings, Alice Ingram usually felt dejectedly sick. She felt desperate enough for sensual emotions. Even now, despite where she was behind the bar at Smiley's, her body screamed for utter fulfillment. She needed to be inside a room where it would be most permissible to quench her bodily thirst. Not that she would lose her bearings, yet the hunger lingered in her flanks, developed and took hold of her flesh. It was like a cancer in her stomach and thighs, and her soul screamed in desperation. Liquor which was available might have done something to ease the persistent craze in her soul, had she not been at work. Yet, hardly to any extent that she would have been utterly relieved. She knew very well that the only remedy for the persistant demands of her body was to be with Eddie. He was her joy, her pleasure, her only love. This morning, more than ever, her soul bled for him. Eddie knew just how to pleasure her, to strip away her terror of loneliness and the persistent headaches which usually accompanied such vague, sensual terrors.

They were engaged, but Eddie hadn't been round to the apartment for three whole days now. Even though he had phoned her, stating that he was working nights and sleeping mostly days during the moments she was at work, thus this hampered them from seeing each other. He had never said what type of work he was doing which kept him away from her. She hated to go around his various gambling haunts in order to hunt him up. Did he mean to stay away from her after becoming engaged to her? Why was she so doubtful about his love? Had the detective, Thomas McShane, been the reason that Eddie had been frightened away from her the past few days? McShane had met them two weeks ago coming from a movie on the Avenue. Frieta, her daughter, had been along. Frieta was twenty-one. McShane hadn't said anything out of the ordinary to Eddie. The detective was an old friend of hers. He'd married her best girl friend, Sophie, after his wife had passed. She and Sophie had come to Kansas from Waco, Texas ten years ago. And had been here ever since. McShane had merely been showing his courtesy to her, not caring who her company was. Eddie acted as if the detective had eyed him for a suspicious reason, afterwards, the way he flushed and kept a hushed mouth. If he wasn't in any trouble why did he shun away from a city cop?

The tavern was practically empty, excepting an old gent seated at the front bar sipping a straight whisky. Smiley, the boss, had been gone since having unlocked the door at eight. He had other businesses and hardly spent any time at the tavern, only at night when business picked up, and on Fridays and Saturdays when business rushed.

The cook was in the kitchen, busily cooking ham and baking off his various meats which sandwiches were made, and the porter, having finished his cleaning out front as well as his bar work, was in the kitchen helping the cook. The other two waitresses who worked at Smiley's wouldn't be on until at noon, so Alice was alone for the time being.

Momentarily, she took a quarter from a pocket of the yellow smock she wore, turned to the counter to one of the music vendors and inserted the money and pressed the button for the song she wanted. Immediately, 'Finally' started playing.

Alice had finished her work and leaned her elbows on the counter, resting her chin in her hands. Riveting baby-blue eyes at the hard rain, she visioned herself curled up in bed in a dingy hotel room with her arms and thighs wrapped tightly round Eddie's dusky body. As the sensual scene struck her her blond flesh flushed and she clenched her fists from the drudgery of having to work every day except Sunday of her life. Working was compulsory in order to live. Unless one was rich. And she was one life span away from that.

At thirty-five, Alice was very attractive, despite the fact that she had lead an unusual life of indulgence. Her blond hair was cropped but reminded one of fabric of silk. Her breasts were small, yet very thrusted and showed somewhat underneath the smock. Her hips were broad, and her buttocks rounded and heavy. She was well stacked, and tempting to any man.

Suddenly a black car cruised up out front. Looking out the side window, Alice saw two men, wearing heavy gray slickers climb out and hurry towards the front door. Coming inside the men flung their coats open and rain splashed on the floor. Without pausing, they crossed over to the bar and took stools.

Alice stared into the pug-nosed, swarthy face of Thomas McShane.

McShane was short and stocky, but his companion was unusually huge and tall, perhaps, six four. While McShane pushed fifty, his partner looked to be thirty-five or more, yet both wore firm, hardened expressions, the strain of detection.

The detective showed no alarm when he saw Alice. She had told him the last time she had seen him where she was working, so his appearance was probably instinctively more than accidentally.

"How'dy, Alice," he said to her, smiling easily. He nodded at his companion. "This is Wayne.... Duke Wayne."

"Hello McShane," she spoke. Then to the big cop. "Please to meet you, Mr. Wayne."

Wayne's fat face beamed with pride as he nodded curtly at her.

Alice pulled two glasses of water and placed them. "What you guys gonna have?" she asked.

"Duke wants a drink," said McShane, nodding at Wayne. "Thought I'd drop in on you for a chat. Here's your gal, Duke."

"You sure pick 'em pretty, Thomas," Wayne said, eyeing Alice's broad hips. "It sure gives me a pleasure to be off duty, so I can be my own judge 'bout livin'. A highball, sugar. Order what you want, pal. On me."

McShane refused a drink. He continued to sip the water as Alice turned to the bar and fixed the highball for Duke. When she handed Duke his drink, he caught her hand and held it. She didn't resist, but wished he'd stop it. A roused feeling in her stomach made her breathless, a little.

"What you doin' tonight, sugar?" Duke asked aggressively.

Alice smiled over at McShane, then rested her eyes on Duke's handsome features. She certainly didn't wish to discourage him. Not tonight, though. Perhaps some other time, when she could be sure Eddie wasn't going to be her man.

She looked past his broad shoulders towards the window at the rain, then back into his light-brown eyes.

"When it rains," she said teasingly, "I like to sleep."

Duke looked at McShane, and they deceived each other.

"So do I, sugar," Duke said. "Maybe we can join each other. Huh?"

"Maybe?" she giggled and turned over to McShane, who laughed outright at their sensual pryings.

"Hows Sophie, McShane?" she asked the detective.

"Right well, Alice," he said. "I told her we met last week or so. Wants you to stop by and see her. No need to stay away because her old man's a cop, is there?"

"You don't keep me away, honey."

"Maybe your boy friend does?" McShane asked more seriously.

She dropped her gaze, thoughtfully.

"What do you mean?" she asked.

"Name's Eddie LaRose, isn't it?" McShane pried.

She nodded suspiciously.

"He's the wrong type of person for you to be associating with, Alice," he advised her.

"You know him?" she asked.

"Sure. Who doesn't here? Had over a dozen or more arrests."

"On what charges?" she inquired nervously.

"Various ones," he smiled. "Don't be frightened. Nothing like murder. Only gambling and a few petty jobs. Nothin' serious. Maybe he'll come out of it."

"Got anything on him now?" she asked.

"Nothing."

"Then he'll be all right," she imagined. "He's working. He's got a job, at night. We're engaged. See." She showed the white-diamond engagement ring to him. McShane took hold of her long-tapering fingers and looked at the diamond. Then he showed it over to Duke. They smiled back at Alice as if it was a joke of some kind.

In order to drop the subject McShane asked, "How's Frieta?"

Alice was still troubled at the detective's cautioning of her with Eddie, but she managed to force a smile.

"She'll do," she said.

"Must be nearly nineteen, by now," he smiled.

"She's twenty-one," Alice informed him.

"Finished college this year?"

"She finished Junior College last year."

"What's she gonna do now?" he asked.

"What's left for her to do?" Alice said. "Wants to be a dancer, and she's taking lessons in singing from a guy named Charley Boyles. He stays up the street from us."

"Frieta always was quite a dancer, even when a tiny kid. Well, we'd better shake. Finished your drink, Duke?"

Duke nodded, dug into his coat pocket and extracted a dollar bill. He placed it on the counter and stood. "What time you get off, Sugar?" he asked, grinning.

"At six," she said, picking up the money.

"I'll drop by 'bout that time," he said.

"Do then. Nasty as this weather is, I sure could stand a lift home."

McShane looked into her eyes before he left the stool. "You're very pretty, Alice," he smiled. "Don't spoil your life. Marry some decent chap who you can depend upon."

Her suspense strangled her. She eyed the engagement ring and looked hard at McShane.

"What have you got against Eddie?" she asked. "What has he done so horrible? I don't care what he's done in the past, I'll stand by him. I'll give my life to help him, McShane. What's he done, so bad, so horrible, now?"

He looked back at the nervous look on her face, shook his head. "Nothing," he said. "Eddie's clean right now. He's nothing but a bum. What he'll do tomorrow? Who knows?"

Alice snarled, her temper had intensified. "All right... all right, you just don't like the guy. Cops never like anybody, anyway. I've been down there. You ought to know that. Every soul, in your opinion, is dirty. Can't reform. Can't be good once dirt's been smeared on you. Well, as long as you don't have a damn thing on Eddie, I needn't worry. Why don't cops trust anybody, once they've been in a little trouble. Nobody's all clear, not even you flawless cops, I'd think. Well, I'm goin' to marry him, see. I'm so crazy about Eddie until I can't think about anybody else but him, right now."

McShane shrugged and left the stool. He flipped a half dollar tip to her on the counter and walked away. When he reached the door, before following Duke out, he turned and looked wearily disgusted back at her.

"Remember I warned you," he said. "I don't have pity for anybody that stubborn. I've only been studying criminals for thirty years. So long Alice."

She waved at him, and he went out the door.

After she had watched their car drive off, she covered her face, feeling depressed for several moments. She could not imagine Eddie as a thief, or robber, or murderer. He treated Frieta and her so kind and gentle. Above all else, he was so loving, so able and young to pleasure her into a contented ecstasy beyond all her dreams. She loved him more so for his sensual moments. Greatly!

Certainly no stupid cop could remind her to break her marriage engagement because of her lover's past morals. She had never found any fault in Eddie, and until she did, she would not suspect anything of him which would disrupt their love and their future plans to marry. Still the detective's words lingered on her mind, and was so annoying upon her conscience until she went back into the rest room and cried.

CHAPTER TWO

FRIETA INGRAM DID NOT get out of bed until half past twelve. When she was before the dresser in the bedroom, she removed her sleeping pajamas and sat naked on the vanity bench. The furnace had come on, due to the extreme cool weather, therefore, the room was very warm and comfortable.

Frieta heard the pounding rain, while studying her nude body in the mirror. She felt numb and unused, wishing she could find something to occupy her interest until she could find a summer job. Drive-ins weren't doing any business because of the raw and uncomfortable weather. She didn't want to be a waitress in any cheap cafe. She hated to think of herself being a two-bit hash slinger, as Alice was.

She picked up a comb and ran it through her shoulder-length, honey-blond hair. Her complexion was smooth, velvet tender skin which she felt proud of. Thank God, she thought, she'd finished Junior College. In two more years she could teach, if Alice could afford to send her off. Yet she could devote her time to her music and ballet. She wasn't going to Charley's to take any lessons today. Too bad. Anyway, she didn't feel in any mood for singing while the day was so lousy and rainy.

Frieta was somewhat identical in her characteristics as her mother. At twenty-one, she knew what she wanted to do about her love. With school out, and no more dates with Junior College boys, she'd have to find her a steady guy to date. She was contemplating marriage, yet she feared it would interfere with her career. Certainly she wanted to enter show business and become famous, and earn a fabulous salary. She could buy a great wardrobe, enjoy herself with other luxuries.

The pattern of ethics which Alice had set before her daughter was not one to be proud of. Frieta had seen her mother drunk more times than she could recall, and often heard her in the bedroom entertaining her gentlemen friends. Frieta felt as if she was old enough to indulge, and she often did. She smoked and drank, but Alice had cautioned her about going any further with her boy friends. Alice had dropped her when she was thirteen, and she did not intend to let her own daughter become pregnant and be jilted and left with a bastard such as that rogue had treated her down in Texas.

After Frieta had combed her hair, she got up off the vanity bench and entered the bathroom. She relieved herself, and re-entered the bedroom to pull her mother's nylon bathrobe round her body. They were practically the same size, only Frieta's breasts were much more developed, hanging heavier but thrusting and beautiful. The girl's hips and thighs were not quite as broad as her mother's, yet they were shapely and trim enough to beautify her body. Her baby-blue eyes were the same color as Alice's, but her thin lips were smiling, without the unsound boredom which Alice usually felt.

Being with appetite, Frieta left the bedroom, passed through a large dining room and entered the kitchen. There she opened the refrigerator, selected ham and eggs and carefully fixed herself a delicious breakfast.

The five room apartment was over an old furniture store at Eighth and Kansas avenue. The front section, a kitchenette, was occupied by Gladys Hernden and her husband, Mike. They were elderly people. Mike had been a mail-carrier before being confined to bed with lung cancer. His wife, Gladys, did not have to work since both drew their pensions, so she merely spent her days in the small quarters caring for her ailing husband. It was a very sad omen, for Mike Hernden was not expected to live more than a month or so. Every day Frieta could hear the old woman singing and praying to her husband. Sometimes their pastor visited them, offering prayers for the inflicted old man.

Upon finishing her breakfast, Frieta returned to the front room and started the record player. She heard someone climbing the stairs, walking heavily along the bare hallway until they were at Gladys's door. There was a knock, and Frieta heard the old woman admitting the doctor. The door slammed shut, and Frieta shrugged and felt sorry for Gladys and her stricken husband. After the doctor left she would visit Gladys and try to console her miserable loneliness.

The music entered her bones. She flung away the nylon robe. Nude, now, she flounced before a mirror embedded in the door leading into the dining room. The syncopation was slow and intriguingly disturbing to her sensuality. Maybe it was the raw day which had penetrated her soul. She felt herself, slowly caressed her breasts. Wishing hopefully, desirously. The pattern formed, delightfully she responded to the emotional feeling which possessed her. Gradually, she trembled, then started undulating her hips. She snapped her fingers in time. What she needed was something to relieve the loneliness she felt, something as she had often heard Alice so desperately after. She needed help. She avoided men. Had to. She knew she was sick, now foolish, and desperate. Must she wait until her marriage to satisfy her constant demands? God, how she felt for something to happen this morning. The rainy mornings and nights tormented her soul, making her desire bleed and demand instant attention.

Frieta felt her hips racing in response to the urgency of her body's demands and her thighs started trembling and she fell down to the floor, placed her legs upon a chair and making little whineful sighs to herself, undulated her hips faster and faster.

The music was unusually loud, and she was so thrilled with her own self-gratification, she failed to hear the footsteps on the stairsteps. A moment later a key was inserted into the door. The door was opened and a tall smooth-faced man stepped into the room and shut the door.

He heard the record player, but was unable to detect anyone for a brief moment.

Eddie LaRose removed a smoking cigarette from his lips as his dark eyes caught sight of Frieta on the opposite side of the room with her feet propped up in the chair. She had heard the door click shut and the noise had cautioned her to halt her self indulgence. She was motionless when Eddie first spied her, still she was naked lying on the floor and her thighs were apart.

Frieta twisted her head and looked shamefaced and guilty round at him. Flushed, and embarrassed, she threw her legs to the floor, reaching, snatched the thin nylon robe to cover herself. Neither of them had spoken. He was too startled to see what he had seen, and she was too shamefaced and guilty to speak.

Frieta sat up on the floor and slipped her arms into the robe, braced herself over against the chair and dropped her gaze down at the floor.

"Hello Frieta," he said. "Hope I'm not intruding?"

Without looking at him, she said, "It's okay. Come on in and rest your things. I never expected nobody. I was exercising. It's sure rainin', isn't it?"

"You bet it is," he said, removing a rain slicker and shaking the water from it. It was not the first time he had seen Frieta's naked body; several instances she had come into the sitting room where he was sitting without a stitch on, only to pretend she was embarrassed upon finding him seated there.

Frieta rose slowly to her feet. Her face was flushed as yet, and her eyes had grown fiery and tender. They appeared wild-ishly disturbed as she met his gaze from across the big room. The record player was still going. Frieta reached and stopped it. The silence was even more disturbing. She was thinking how it would be with him. For a long time, now, she had felt that way towards Eddie. Often she coveted him, and found herself despising her mother for having met him first. Sometimes he kissed her, only mere childish kisses, as a father would, but the kisses were enough to create a vague hollow in the pit of her belly, and she could not sleep throughout the night.

Facing him again, she eased over to a sofa chair, dropped into it and picked up a cigarette lying on the end table. A match was there and she lit the cigarette and smoked.

He smiled down at her, then crossed the room and entered the bathroom where he placed his dripping rain slicker in the bath tub to drain off.

Once again in the front room with her she noticed that he wore a new light-gray suit and new light-tanned slippers. He possessed a different air then when she had last seen him. He looked proud, as though he had accomplished something very substantial enough to make him somebody. He had a fresh haircut, and shave, and his complexion was smooth along his rounded cheeks. He had a massage. His entire body seemed to give off a pleasing sweetness, the refreshed odor of after visiting the barbershop.

"Where's Alice?" he asked.

"Working," she said, allowing cigarette smoke to curl from her lips. She blushed up at him, but he didn't notice her. He was six feet, blackhaired, dark eyes, square chin and lean cheeks. He didn't have any book learning, but he seemed very romantically inclined. Eddie knew how to love a woman. She knew that. Alice had told her how nice and sweet he was. All girls knew what that meant. Alice had stated that Eddie was the sweetest lover she had ever had and she could hardly stand him out of her sight.

Frieta felt that the man didn't love her mother. He was twenty-five, ten years younger than Alice. There was little doubt in Frieta's mind that he didn't have other girls on Alice. In her suspiciousness she felt that was why he didn't come round as often as he should have. Any man who was engaged to her would certainly have to see her every night when he wasn't working.

Eddie came whenever he felt like it. He may not show up for a week, or even two weeks. In her opinion he did not want Alice, even after boasting about his great love and devotion to her.

Eddie, lighting a fresh cigarette, remained standing near the television.

"Alice was worried about you," Frieta reminded him. "She's half crazy, wondering why you didn't show up?"

He smiled. "I phoned, and told her I was workin'. A guy has to work, sugar."

She eyed him deeply, noticing his new garb again. "I guess so," she said. "You're all dressed up. Where you workin', Eddie?"

"Gambling, sugar."

"Three days and nights?"

"Sure. Long as there's guys with dough, and cards with aces, and dice with sevens, I win. So I keep playin', see."

"You were lucky?"

Instead of answering her, he felt into his pants pocket and extracted a huge roll of greenbacks. All Frieta could see were twenties and tens and fives.

"Was I!" he sighed proudly.

"How much you win, Eddie?" Her lips lay apart, her eyes bulged at the sight of all the money.

"Two-thousand bucks, sugar," he answered, tossing the roll upon the divan.

Frieta rose from her chair, taking pains to clasp the nylon robe so it would not flap open. The room was very obscure so it was hardly possible for Eddie to see through the thin garment. Still she felt somewhat uncomfortable before him, dressed so scantily.

She leaped over to the divan and started counting the money. He stood back, proudly smoked and watched her count.

Excitedly, Frieta counted the money for nearly ten minutes. It was every bit of two-thousand dollars, and a few dollars to add. He had bought clothes and visited the barbershop.

When she had finished counting the money, she crossed her legs and eyed him enviously.

"What you gonna do with all this dough?" she asked with a tender giggle.

"Buy a car," he said. "Buy plenty liquor, and have a ball. I might even get married."

"Won't Alice be happy."

"Maybe we three can celebrate," he said. "She can lay off the job a week and rest. Alice needs rest. She works too damn hard for a few lousy bucks at that goddamned tavern. What time does she get off?"

"At six," she stated. She looked up at him and blushed. "You hungry, Eddie? I'll fix you some ham and eggs, if you are."

"Nothin' doin', sugar. I'm gonna take me a drink and sleep myself away." He removed his coat, felt into one pocket and extracted a fifth of whisky. He tossed the coat across a chair and dropped down on the divan beside her and the money. He unscrewed the cap off the whisky bottle, handed her the bottle.

"There, Frieta, take a drink on Eddie LaRose."

She took the bottle and raised it to her lips and took a nice drink with him. She felt the burning sensation as the whisky cut into her belly and stirred her insides into warmer emotions. She handed him the bottle back, watched him a moment, as he tilted the fifth to his lips and took a gulping drink. Then she rose and keeping the robe tightly round her body, she crossed over to a side window and looked out at the darkness and the threatening rain. Lightning flashed now, and thunder rumbled. The old apartment building was jarred. Frieta dropped the curtains and turned back to the record player. She started the same record she had played before. The music went through her. Haunted by desire again, she crossed back over to the divan and sat down beside Eddie, drawing her legs underneath her body so she would not be to blame for his emotions becoming disturbed.

He was studying her, now. His dark eyes penetrated the front of the nylon robe, and it wasn't the yellow color of the material which had beset his eyes. It was the coned shape of her thrusting breasts. The very bulge of her nipples showed plainly, and he parted his thick lips, lusting after her.

He looked down at the money, and grinned. Then he took another drink, and still another. He wasn't talking, now. Just watching the money and drinking. Frieta smoked again. She eyed the money with all kinds of thoughts created in her mind. With all that money she could make Vivian and Stella and Beatrice, her school chums insanely jealous of her. She could buy the kind of clothes which she had always wanted. She could become even more beautiful than she was. What would Charley Boyles, her voice teacher, think of her if he saw her wearing patent leather high heels and a white satin dress and her hair marcelled? God, she'd be the envy of Kansas Avenue. All the poor suckers would stare and stare like lustful puppies.

When the fifth of whisky was nearly half empty, Eddie placed it on the table to the right of the divan and reached for the money. He gathered all the greenbacks up and held them between his long fingers. Suddenly, he looked at Frieta, and said,

"Come here, Frieta."

She edged over beside him. He took her into his arms and kissed her lips. Then she pulled back. She eyed him carefully, trying to imagine just how serious he was, or if it was merely a loving caress as he would a child. Her breath intensified, and her lips trembled. She had to escape him before she acted indecent. She was already dressed indecent before him. She wasn't intending to become an easy woman for any man. Not like Alice. Alice gave and gave, openly, freely, easily. She was definitely a push-over.

The whisky stirred Frieta again. The burning created an unfulfilled desire in her flanks. She stirred uneasily beside Eddie. Still she watched him very carefully, especially his dark lusty eyes.

Whatever was on her mind he seemed to be able to understand. He smiled again and peeled off five hundred dollars and tossed it into her lap. She looked down at the money and back up at him.

"What's that for?" she asked quickly. Her own voice betrayed her. Hers was a foul tone, anxiously excited.

He dropped his bottom lip, then reached and caressed her left knee.

"Just try to imagine, baby," he said, and lifted his stare at her lips again. Her lips trembled.

Frieta stared down at the money again, then looked back up at him. She blushed, felt her breasts quiver, and her throat was dry. Her heart throbbed. She was uneasily excited.

Her gesture was involuntary. Quickly, she brushed the money away. It fell over against the divan cushion. She looked at him, then dropped her gaze as she very well realized what he wanted from her, by now. She wanted to get up and leave, enter the bedroom and slam the door in his face. He was Alice's beau, and she dare not betray her own mother. Alice might find out some way, or would she?

He realized what her drawback was. He meant to console her, to remedy her puzzled expression.

"Listen, Frieta," he said, leaning towards her. "I love you, sugar. For over six months I've wanted to tell you, sugar. Please, it's the truth. I'm not lyin'. Alice, why, she's too old for me. You know that. I'm just twenty-five. Don't you reckon she's too old for me?"

She didn't answer. Her lips were parted, and her mind was befuddled and confused.

"I'm tryin' to think of how to break it to Alice," he went on, speaking very bluntly, though his words were stilted, as the liquor was working on his system.

"Honest, I'm sorry," he went on. "My God, she's gonna nearly die when I tell her, but that's th' way it is. I can't marry her. I can't. I just can't. I wouldn't be faithful, I wouldn't be true."

"You've got to marry her," she blurbed. "You're engaged."

"I'll speak to her. I'll tell her that I'm in love with you. Alice ain't no fool. She'll understand. She's got to understand!"

She started to get up, to leave him, to order him out of the apartment, but he caught her arm and detained her action. She waited, tenderly gentle to his touch.

Slowly Eddie picked up the five hundred dollars, and to this amount he added another five hundred, making it a thousand. He tossed it into her lap, and watched the expression come over her face.

"What's that for?" she swallowed again. "Eddie, that's a thousand dollars! You givin' it all to me?"

"Sure."

"What do I have to do?"

"What do you think?"

"No …. no! Alice might find out!" She looked at him, hoping he would not agree with her. And he didn't.

"Who's goin' to tell her?"

She looked into his hard eyes, but could find no answer. She dropped her gaze again at the money, thinking how easy it was to earn. So easy, so enjoyably easy. So sensationally easy, so heavenly, so sweet, so deliciously soothing to her soul. To be paid over a thousand dollars just to pleasure him, to pleasure herself as well. He would be the one cheated, not her. Only her conscience to disturb her, after. And such would hardly hurt, since he had said that he wasn't going to marry Alice anyway. That would be their fight, not hers. After he had broken with Alice, she could have him all to herself. After all, wasn't he the man she wanted, desired, and was thinking about a moment ago when sex self-stimulated herself?

Slowly her right hand reached for the money. Then both hands gathered up all the greenbacks. She looked at him as she lifted the sofa cushion and thrust the money underneath it. He was taking another drink. When he finished the drink, he looked at her and placed the bottle back on the table.

Frieta pushed herself back on the divan, waiting, her lips parted, her heart throbbing.

He saw that she had fallen for his enticement. Any girl would. He knew what their bait was. Money. She was in his web. So young and tender, so ripe, so innocent. She would go crazy about him, and he would certainly become a lunny about her. Frieta was beautiful, very graceful and enticing. Madly he moved over towards her.

As he came over to her, his right hand slipped away the nylon robe and peeled it off. Her eyes were frightened and nervous, at first. She watched him remove his clothes, shuck down, until he was stripped just as she was. The music was still playing. She blinked lustily when he stood before her and she saw the shape and size of him. She gasped, fell back on the divan and waited until he was upon her. She parted; one leg he lifted upon the back of the divan. She sneered as he pressed, feeling her with one finger. She was no virgin. A high school boy, whom she had been dating during her junior year had taken her virginity one night in the bottom hallway when he had brought her home after a basketball game.

"I needed someone!" she moaned, as he kissed her left breast and the sensation surged through her body. She clutched at him, inhaling his masculine body, feeling his hot lips sulking her, slowly her flanks crawled higher and higher.

"You're a hot blooded little bitch!" he sighed sensually. "Now?" he said.

She flattened herself against his body, feeling his scratching hairs of his chest against her breasts. Her own fingers slid down between them, past his stomach until he felt her fingers grip his hard flesh. She gave a rigid soothing rasp of her lips as she pressed herself and twisted up gradually until he had her. Her body stiffened, and flushed as waves of contraction gripped her. Her legs tightened on him.

"Take me!" she cried. "Do it fast, Eddie.... make me hurt ... make me cry ...." She demanded in a tone contrary to any he had ever heard admitted by a girl in the position she was in.

He pleasured her until she felt herself undulating her hips wildly and uncontrollably. In dripping perspiration, her flesh dimpled and burned to his endless heavenly torment.

At last her body made several wild convulsions, and she threw her arms to both sides and screamed in his face and he screamed in her face. Then they fell against one another and kissed and caressed each other until he had fallen asleep.

A moment later Frieta was under the shower, when the phone rang. With dripping water she ran into the front room to answer it. It was Alice. She wouldn't be home until after two. One of the waitresses didn't show up for work, so she had to work two shifts. Upon inquiring whether Eddie had been there, Frieta lied, and stated that he hadn't.

When she had dressed and pulled on a rain cape, Frieta entered the front room and looked down at her drunkardly sleeping paramour. She fetched a blanket from the bedroom and covered him up on the divan. Stooping, she placed a firm, sincere kiss on his lips.

"Eddie, honey," she sighed contemplatively. "I love you, honey. I love you! I love you!"

His feet were resting on the divan cushion, but she lifted them, removed the cushion and retrieved the thousand dollars. As she crammed all the money into a scratched, worn black purse, one which Alice had loaned her to use, she sighed with anticipation of all the wonderful things which she was going to buy herself.

She kissed Eddie again, then turned towards the door. She would not have to worry about Alice returning home and finding Eddie asleep on the divan, since she wouldn't be coming home until after two A. M. Right now, she was going downtown and buy herself a lot of pretty clothes, and then flounce herself before the whole town!

Frieta opened the door and left the room. She was not interested in visiting Gladys Hernden, now. She was far too entranced in her vanity pleasures to visit the sick, on woman.

CHAPTER THREE

IT WAS NEARLY SIX in the evening before Frieta returned to the apartment heavily laden with packages, consisting of hat boxes, shoe boxes, underclothing, hose, a green purse, another brown one and a purple handbag.

Rain was still falling, but not quite as hard as it had been. She came into the front room and dumped all her new things upon the empty divan, because Eddie had moved. He was in the kitchen, not so drunk as he had been before she had left for town. He was cooking meat balls and spaghetti, his special dish. The pleasant aroma reminded Frieta that she hadn't eaten since breakfast.

Before she could reach the kitchen door he was blocking her path, dressed in trousers, wearing one of Alice's tie aprons. He grinned, very handsome, he took her into his arms. They kissed. Her own hands clawed at his shoulders. She felt that special part of him again, growing rigid, stiffly against her body. She wanted to pull him into the bedroom this time, but fearful that Alice might not work the second shift, after all, quenched the idea, and also, made a sense of dread overwhelm her pending desires.

"Gee," she sighed, brushing him aside, "that smells delicious, Eddie." She looked over at the kitchen table. Plates had been set, knives and forks and spoons. For three. He didn't know that Alice wouldn't be there. Perhaps his idea was to tell her about them after they had eaten. Alice would be able to digest their guilt much better on a full stomach.

He was looking back towards the divan where she had placed all her purchases. Then he turned back to her, somewhat pleased at her buying spree. It gave him a lift to be able to make such a pretty young girl happy.

She was washing her hands at the sink, now, readying herself to eat. He was still watching her, his dark eyes glued to the curves of her hips, the slant of her complete figure. He was gloating at her as if he could not believe he had seen her without any clothes on, and not to speak of having pleasured her.

When she turned back to the table and pulled back a chair to sit down he was still standing at the door wearing a nervous expression. Their eyes met, and she giggled, because he looked so funny, as if he was completely lost.

"What's th' matter, Eddie?" she asked. "Are you sick?"

"Hardly, sugar. I was thinkin'. I got to think right good, now for sure. Don't you reckon?"

She sat down at the table and placed the knife on the right side; he had been careless.

"I don't know," she said. "What's so deep that you can't figure out?"

"Us."

"You can skip it, honey," she told him. "If your food's ready, give a starved gal something to eat. Alice phoned to say that she wouldn't be coming home until morning."

His face lifted. He was relieved, somewhat. "How come?" he asked.

She giggled again. "She's working another shift. Rose, the other waitress, never showed up. Come on, honey. Let's eat."

After they had eaten, they washed dishes together and cleaned up the kitchen. Later they retired into the front room.

Frieta spent the next hour opening her new things and putting them on for him to see and comment on how she looked in them. She modeled for him, and was flattered by his constant praise in her taste and her preference to women's wear.

When he was tired of watching her display, he mentioned for her to hide everything from Alice until they could think of a plan to tell her just how they felt towards each other. Frieta gathered all her things, replacing them into their respective boxes, and concealed them under the bed out of Alice's eyesight.

At a quarter to eight, she had shed her clothes and donned a lavender nylon robe of her own, which she had just purchased. Eddie was outstretched on the divan. He was drinking again.

She dropped down across his lap, embracing his shoulders, kissing him deeply, while his tapering fingers crawled along her left thigh and felt like crabs along her naked flesh.

"Do you really love me, Eddie?" she asked spitefully. "I'm thinking that you just bought me this afternoon."

"I'm mad after you, Frieta. Plain mad. No dame's worth a thousand bucks. Don't you know that. When I give that much to a skirt, well, she's got me by the neck. I'm under her yoke. I'll bleed and sweat for her. Maybe, even, die."

She giggled from his words, which seemed more poetic than plain reasoning. She kissed him, and pressed her tongue between his lips and caused them to part so she could tongue him, a little. Most teenagers kissed that way. It made the feeling come. Made her giddy, almost squirm in his lap. She loved it and needed it. She felt herself wasted so many days, here alone with nothing to do. Now this was living. She must not louse up such rewarding sweetness. Here was something which pleased her. made time stop, or slip past faster. She didn't care which. In a man's arms, a big man's arms.

"When you gonna tell Alice?" she inquired. "Tonight? Or tomorrow, or when?"

"I'm goin' for a walk tonight," he said. "Can't see her before tomorrow. Won't that be time enough, sugar?"

"Sure. I reckon. Only, where're you goin'? I thought we could … oh, please, Eddie!"

His fingers were between her thighs, making her twist, tremble and squirm on his lap. Fire leaped into the pit of her stomach. Her lips parted. She thrust her mouth to his. Madly her fingers clawed at his hair.

"Please, Eddie …. please!"

He got the message. He picked her up and carried her through the doorway into the bedroom. There he placed her gently on the bed. He stood back and smiled at her. His dark eyes were devilish, somewhat bloodstained. He managed to get his trousers off, while she found her own fingers fumbling with the nylon robe to remove it from her body. He turned out the light. Thoughts of darkness stimulated the thrill in her, created a savage lust in her which she had never felt before.

As she felt him beside her, she quickly parted her legs and felt her flesh grow numb as he contacted her. Sweetness poured through her veins. Her flanks quivered, and she lifted herself more, eager. Her buttocks flattened against his hands, and her hips raced with incredible energy as he matched her wild pace.

At two-thirty A.M. he was gone. He had left two hours before, stating he had to get in a card game somewhere near Fifth and Osage. She didn't question him. He had worn her out, given her a sound working over. She felt gentle and possessed. Her fire had smouldered. Her demanding thirst was quenched, well satisfied.

Frieta lay wide awake. It was hardly possible for her to sleep, knowing that she was too madly in love with Eddie to five. She had begged him to take her with him, but he had refused. There was no need to make matters any worse than they already were. After all, Alice at least, deserved a break.

Alice came home at two-forty. Frieta heard her slow footsteps on the stairs, and in order to pretend she was asleep, she turned her head to the wall and covered her head with the covers. She was in her own room, and Alice wouldn't bother to wake her. Her guilt was too compelling to confront her mother. It was better for her to pretend sleep.

Alice unlocked the door, turned on the front room light and flung her handbag on the divan. She gave a tired sigh, as if the sixteen hours of drudgery she had put in at Smiley's had just about murdered her. The detective had not picked her up at six because she had to work the second shift, so Smiley had driven her home after the joint had closed.

Alice shed her rain cape, shoes and skirt. Then she walked over to Frieta's room door, opened it, turned on the light to see if her daughter was in.

Indeed Frieta was home. The covers were tucked snugly about her shoulders, and Alice assumed she was sound asleep. So she turned out the light and closed the door.

Back in the front room again, she flung herself on the divan and lit a cigarette. She wondered if Eddie had showed up, and since there was nothing to give her a cue that he had, she assumed that he hadn't. Frieta had made certain that all his cigarette butts and his whisky bottle were thrown in the trash out of her mother's eyesight.

When Alice had finished smoking the cigarette, she undressed right in the front parlor. She wished for a drink, and was angry at herself for refusing a bottle of gin which the cook had offered to buy for her to take home. She had refused that fat sonofabitch on purpose, she thought. He was always feeling her tits, and brushing against her real as if she was a whore. She knew well enough what he was after, without all his shimming round and pestering her like a goof. She had a better set-up than that bastard, she imagined. Eddie was young, not in his fifties like the old cook. She wanted a young man who didn't have to plead with himself when the time was ripe.

Alice gave a hard sigh, discontented, of course. Then she peeled off the last of her garments, leaving them lay, on the divan. She was nude when she crossed the room to the light switch. She turned out the light and entered her own bedroom. She turned on a light, saw that Frieta had done nothing to her bed, nor the room, and with a disgusted sigh, turned the light back out and crawled into the bed with the sickening thought of having to get back up at eight to return to work again.

"Goddamn my life," she swore. She wanted to feel sorry for herself, but she dare not become so feeble-minded. She had tried time after time to meet some guy who would be decent enough to marry her and give her a nice home. That was all she wanted out of life, a decent guy to be true and honest to her. Always, despite how nice and kind she was to her lovers, she seemed to get the raw deal. How was she to ever break such ugly vicissitudes of life which always plunged her welfare and desires into such defeatism?

Alice was exhaustedly tired, having been on her feet all through the day. She had hardly lain down before she was sound asleep.

CHAPTER FOUR

WHEN FRIETA AWAKENED the next morning and left her own bedroom to make a survey of the apartment, she found Alice already gone. An electric clock on the T.V. said, ten A. M.

Frieta washed up, combed her hair and dressed in a pair of jeans. She wondered why Alice didn't call her as she usually did just before leaving for work. She concluded that her mother was obviously late, having to double back so early again.

Thank God the weather had cleared for once. The sunny morning added brightness to her spirits. Above all, she felt as if she wanted to dress up and make another buying spree. Only this morning, after she had taken her singing lessons, she was going to the beauty parlor and get herself a permanent. When Eddie saw her that afternoon she would be beautiful enough for anything. She wanted him to take her to a night-club, or a downtown movie. Alice might be home at six, but she hoped they would be gone by that time. She imagined that if Eddie dodged Alice long enough, her mother might become disgusted with their engagement and break it herself. Frieta was definitely going to mention it to Eddie when he came.

After having a nice breakfast of hot coffee, buttered toast, bacon and eggs, Frieta busied herself cleaning up the entire apartment. She knew Alice would raise hell if she returned home another day and found things in a filthy mess as such had been the past day.

She did not finish with the cleaning work until noon. By then she was very hungry again. The television was going, and Frieta was about to fix herself a light snack for lunch when a knock came at the door.

She hustled over to open the door, hoping to God it was Eddie.

It was Gladys Hernden.

Wearing a soiled greenish kimono and shabby house-slippers, Gladys smiled deeply and wobbled into the front room and closed the door.

"Mornin', Frieta," the old woman said.

"Oh, hello, Gladys," Frieta said. "Sit down. I was just about to fix a bite for lunch. Care for anything?"

Gladys refused. "No, baby. I'm not very much for eatin' this time of day. Been up half the night with Mike." Gladys moved to a sofa chair and sat down. Her graying brunette hair was tousled, something like a wild nest. Her gray eyes were tired, and her thick cheeks sagged greatly out of proportion with her bulbous nose. She was a Christian woman, and was very helpful to Frieta and Alice. While she was past sixty-five, she treated the mother and daughter as though they were her own children.

"Oh, that poor Mike," Frieta moaned in sympathy. "He's just suffering so much." Frieta sat down opposite Gladys, deciding that the lunch could wait. She hadn't seen Gladys for two days and she was just dying for a conversation. None of her girl friends had called since school had let out.

"Doc Fanny was by yesterday," said Gladys. "Didn't give Mike any relief to see him, though. How's Alice?"

"Okay. She worked until two this morning. Had to go right back at eight."

"No wonder I missed her. She usually stops by at six, when she gets off. I wondered why she never stopped yesterday. She still plannin' on marrying that guy, Eddie?"

Frieta had hoped she wouldn't bring up that particular subject. It really hurt her to discuss Eddie's marrying anybody, except her. Even her mother made her jealous, despite the fact that he had said he wasn't going to marry her.

"I really don't know," Frieta replied, blushing. She dropped her gaze, reached for a cigarette lying on the coffee stand. She struck a match and lit the cigarette, offering Gladys one. The old lady shook her head, no smoke for her.

Gladys nodded gingerly as if it didn't matter with her one way or the other, whether Alice married Eddie LaRose or not. Then she said,

"What you gonna do, since you've stopped your education?" Gladys inquired off handedly.

"Oh, I don't know. Loaf mostly, until something happens. I'd like to try for a career, though. Which reminds me, I haven't studied one note on my singing for three whole days. Hell, I won't know a damn thing today."

"You takin' lessons today?"

"Sure am. I'd better be getting ready too. Due there at one-thirty. Charley raises all kinds of hell if any of his students are a minute late. He's worse than going to class."

"Well, I hope Alice drops by this evenin'. I'm gonna make some ginger cookies later on, and I'll give her a batch. She always likes them. You gonna stop by and see Mike before you leave, baby?"

"Of course, Gladys," Frieta said.

"All right, I'll expect you, then." Gladys rose and went towards the door. After Frieta had seen her to her own apartment, she wheeled towards the bathroom to spruce herself up.

It was nearly one in the afternoon before she knocked on Glady's door and entered the large bedroom where she spied Mike on the bed with his body greatly decrepit and eyes deeply sunken in his head. He looked very feeble, and he didn't seem to know Frieta when she spoke to him and gave him her respect.

"Goodness, baby!" Gladys exclaimed. "Where'd you swipe all those new duds. My ... my, you sure look beautiful!"

Frieta wore new heels, white skirt and blue blouse, and carried a new hand bag. She had spent three-hundred dollars, and had hidden five-hundred in the bedroom in her dresser drawer. The remaining two-hundred was in her handbag now; she intended to go shopping for a necklace set after she left voice practice.

Frieta did not tarry long with Gladys Hernden. She called a taxi-cab, and when the cabbie arrived she ran down the stairs and entered the car and told the driver to take her to Eighth and Barnett, to the Goodwell Apartment building. Charley Boyles' rooms were there. His studio was in his front parlor.

Charley Boyles was waiting for her the moment she stepped into the large studio room. He was a tall, calm-faced man with a neat black mustache and long heavy sideburns. His hair was black, though bushy, somewhat unkempt. He usually wore a loud-colored robe. Today he wore a deep maroon robe. He looked very handsome to Frieta.

"Aw, Frieta, my girl," he said, greeting her, as she stepped into the room and he closed the door behind her. "You are right on time. I have just dismissed my little girl, Amanda Kemp. She's such a studious one. Talented, too. Come. We must get started immediately. I have an appointment at two, so you'll have to be dismissed earlier than usual. Okay?"

She smiled up at him. "Sure. I don't know anything, anyway." Her lips longed for his, savoringly.

He eyed her indifferently, then crossed over the room to the right side and dropped down on a piano bench before an ivory-low boy. He tickled the keys, then gave Frieta a pitch. He went over the scale with her, up and down, up and down. Then she had to sing several Contralto allegros. Her voice was much better than it had been. Charley did not know to what extent he could blame for her unusual toned-up efforts. She ended her voice lessons by singing, the "Saint Louis Blues."

When Frieta was finished with her lessons, Charley Boyles offered to drive her downtown, since he was going that way. He had proposed to her, but she had refused. She didn't think he could pleasure her enough. If he had been thirty, she might have been vamped, greatly stirred into becoming infatuated with him. Charley's wife had died the previous year, and he didn't even have a girl friend, yet. She had been taking lessons for nearly two years from Charley. Still she felt more close to him than she did to any other man she knew. He lived her world; she lived his.

Frieta had hardly left the apartment before Alice returned back home at two. She had asked permission for the afternoon off, since working a double shift the day before, and it was granted. She was intending to look Eddie up. The suspense was driving her to distraction. One thing she must take care of her sensual thrist. She just had to find Eddie, or else go stone mad.

At the apartment she shed her dress and kicked off tight high-heels. She had brought a quart of liquor. She extracted the bottle of liquor from her purse, dropped down on the divan. She tore the cap off the bottle and took a hard drink. After a heavy sigh, she took another drink, then felt that it was time to stop for a while.

Looking about the apartment she saw that Frieta had cleaned up very well. Everything was spic and span. She guess Frieta had gone to take her music lessons, knowing it to be the day.

When her spirits had abated, she went to the phone and started dialing numbers, places where Eddie hung around, saloons, pool halls, the rooming house where he lived on Eighteenth street. No one had seen him. His landlord stated that he hadn't been there in three days. Alice gave up after nearly an hour of phoning. It was hard for her to acknowledge that he would deceive her so drastically. Certainly he must have phoned last night while Frieta was home? He never phoned the tavern, like he had at first. Had Eddie really jilted her? Had Thomas McShane been right, after all? She sweated at the sickness which seized her loins. Her demands were even worse than they had been the previous day. She felt a headache coming on. Her soul yearned and screamed for bodily attention. These lonely demons would not let her rest. Unfortunately, she did not know Duke Wayne's telephone number. She felt like giving him a ring. She needed someone. Any man, she felt, who was healthy and respectable enough, might fulfill her ghastly demands. She was becoming more inhuman than ever, as the loneliness lingered and hounded her insides. She needed attention, and she must have it before the day was done!

Alice climbed to her feet and crossed the room to the door to the hallway. She opened the door and left the room. In the dingy hallway, she crossed over to Gladys's door, and knocked. She entered the bedroom to the old lady's greeting.

"Hello, Gladys," Alice spoke. "You feelin' right bad, Mike?"

Mike grunted a weak reply which didn't encourage his feelings any, and Gladys spoke, then hurried to Alice and led her towards a chair beside the kitchen table where she was busy rolling out ginger cookies.

"I'm makin' some ginger cookies," Gladys said. "How you been, Alice? You sure look worn out. Ain't you feelin' well, honey?"

"I feel like hell," Alice said. "God, have you noticed whether Eddie LaRose came to the door when nobody was there, Gladys?"

"No. No. Not that I know of. Frieta was home all day yesterday. I heard the record player goin', but the doctor was here, and Mike was sick so I never got over to see her. I was by your place this mornin'. Frieta and I talked. She was here just before leavin' to take her voice lessons. Never mentioned that guy of yours, though. She sure was dressed fit to kill, Frieta was. You musta got lucky. Did you win some money?"

Alice frowned, thoughtfully. What on earth was Gladys talking about?

"What're you talkin' 'bout?" she asked. "I'm flat broke. Pay day is three days off. You say Frieta was all dolled up?"

"Sure was. New shoes, skirt, blouse, handbag, and God knows what else. She sure looked pretty and sweet."

"Where'd she get money to buy all that outfit?" Alice grimaced, curiously.

Gladys shugged. "Don't know. Never thought to ask her. Don't reckon she's stuck somebody up, do you?"

"She must have. How else would she get so many new things. Frieta don't work. She don't know what it means to get out and look for a job. Somethin's goin' on, that I don't know 'bout. Goddamn her. She'd better not be doin' other things!"

Gladys stopped rolling out the cookies, stared hard at Alice.

"You don't think she's got men friends?"

Alice shrugged, not caring to discuss such a disheartening situation before her nosey neighbor. She was sullenly impatient as she watched Gladys roll out the cookies, and didn't have too much more to say for the next hour that she was there. While Gladys talked about church and a lot of other tripe which didn't have any effect on her, Alice thought about Frieta and the new clothes.

A half hour later she heard Frieta's light footsteps hurrying up the stairs. She would not think Alice was home. It was a little after four.

Alice scraped back her chair and stood. Listening intently, she heard Frieta insert her key in the lock and the door whined open.

"There's Frieta now," Alice said to the old woman. "I'd better get over there and see what this's all 'bout."

She hurried out the room, and crossed the hallway before Frieta could get the door shut. Frieta's eyes nearly popped out when she saw Alice had been home from work already.

"Mama," Frieta said, "you're home early?"

Alice slammed the door and leaned against it, staring up and down at Frieta's new outfit, her sweeping hair-do, and a new set of dangling gold earrings and a necklace to match which looked to have cost nearly a hundred dollars.

"You bet I'm home early," Alice said.

Frieta had dropped two suit boxes on the divan. She flushed and felt herself grow sick, suddenly. She groped for a lie which she felt would stick with Alice.

"What's all this, Frieta?" Alice asked. "Seems you've made yourself a killin'? Where'd all th' dough come from? You sure never got everything on credit, and maybe not just your looks!"

Frieta stared into her mother's undaunted eyes, her flushed face growing darker. She fought for the correct explanation. Yet she already sensed the angry stare in Alice's nervous eyes.

"I just came from Charley's," Frieta said.

"Sure. Of course you did. You had music lessons. Not yesterday, you didn't, though. You was here all day. Gladys said so. Where'd all th' dough come from? You wore new duds today, so you must have gone out to town yesterday in order to buy them. That means you must have gotten the dough yesterday?"

"Charley gave the money to me!" She said it before she could govern herself.

Alice lit a cigarette and smoked.

"How much?" she asked.

"Well, enough to buy these things."

"The earrings and necklace, too?" Alice reached over and lifted the necklace, felt of it.

"Right expensive, tricklets," she surmised. "Charley never put out anything like that on his wife. Since when did he start makin' so much dough that he's got to start spendin' it on his students? Why, you've been floatin' in greenbacks, dearie!"

Frieta frowned at her, then dropped her head. Impulsively, she caught her shoulders and turned her head away from her mother. Alice realized she was lying. The girl's lips were trembling, and she was biting her lips, tears formed in her eyes.

"I hope what I'm thinkin' ain't true," Alice reminded her. "I ain't gonna stand for no goings on as that, Frieta."

Frieta's head snapped round, her eyes blazed. Despite her guilt, she had grown bitter and affronted.

"What're you talkin' about, mama?" she demanded contemptuously. "I haven't done anything. I haven't done anything!"

"Liar. You're lyin', Frieta!"

"I'm not either lying! I'm not! I'm not, I tell you!"

"Stop screamin' at me."

"You're screaming at me. You're accusing me of things... of bad things, maybe!"

"Bad or not. Whatever it is, I'm goin' to get to the bottom of it."

"What're you going to do?" Frieta was nervously upset now.

"Goin' to just phone Charley and ask him if he gave you any money. It's just as simple as that Frieta. If he did, I'm sorry. He ought to be able to clear things up for us. I don't reckon he's tryin' to vamp you, bein' he's old enough for your father. Besides, Charley's too modest. He's no cradle snatcher. I've known him for several years. He's trustworthy, and honest, and decent. I'm afraid he wouldn't ever do a thing like I'm thinkin'."

"What're you thinking, mama?" Frieta was nauseated with dread. "What're you thinking, about me?"

"You know damn well what I'm thinkin'," Alice replied, mashing the cigarette out, and moving towards the phone. "I'll call him, now."

"He isn't home. He had to go downtown!"

"I'll phone anyway. He may be back by now."

"You think I'm having men, don't you. Going to bed with men... men... men! Is that what, Alice...? Is it! I'm a first class filthy slut, huh? Is that what I am, Alice Ingram? Is that what you're takin' me to be... just like you!"

The words were hardly out of her mouth before Alice had bounded across the room and slammed her hand into Frieta's mouth. The girl's head jerked back, her mouth was twisted and she fell over against the divan. Alice reached to grab her by the hair, jerked her roughly to her feet and shoved her towards her bedroom.

"Get outa my sight before I half kill you!" Alice snarled indignantly. "What's gotten into you, speakin' to me that way?"

Crying drastically, Frieta stumbled towards her bedroom door, entered the room and slammed the door shut. She flung herself down on the bed and cried louder than she had at first.

Alice snatched up another cigarette and lit it quickly. She smoked hurriedly, contemplatively as thoughts whirled through her mind. In her disturbed conscience, she forgot to phone Charley. Instead, the phone rang. She answered it. It was Eddie LaRose. He had intended to hear Frieta's voice, but Alice was just as well with him. He had purchased a used car. A green Ford. He was coming by to take her and Frieta out riding.

CHAPTER FIVE

W HEN EDDIE HAD PHONED and stated that he was coming by in a car to taken her out riding, Alice completely dismissed Frieta's predicament. She dressed quickly and hurried downstairs to the lower hallway to wait for Eddie. It was a blessing that he should show up at a particular time when she was about to explode on her daughter. She loved Frieta, and did not want her to be the type of girl which she had become. While she felt that she wasn't to blame for the type of life she had to live, there was some way which she could stop it. It always seemed that the fellows she always met were those with no ambition, regular ass hunters, she guessed.

She smoked as she waited for Eddie, and felt mentally disturbed for slapping Frieta so hard. She did not put too much confidence in her child. Now days the kids were subject to do just about anything if the parents were not there to watch carefully, or to at least offer them the best of corrections. She had failed in correcting Frieta. While she wanted to be decent and live according to the moral standards, she definitely couldn't. She supposed she was just a weakened degenerate who couldn't be helped.

The moment Alice saw the green Ford pull up before the apartment building, she knew it was Eddie. She clutched the collar of her spring coat round her neck, shoved the hallway door open and hurried out to the car.

It had clouded up again. Rain threatened. A stiff wind blew from the north. The weather had hardly warmed up any while the sun had lingered. It was very cool and unpleasant for the month of June.

Eddie smiled when Alice opened the front door and climbed in the car beside of him.

"Where's Frieta?" he wanted to know. "I thought she was home?"

Alice leaned and kissed him on the lips. As she sat back, staring hard at his handsome features, feeling her throbbing heart, she tried to control herself as best she could. Desire surged into her soul. Her stomach felt warm, intensified with a lust for fulfillment.

"Frieta is home," she told him.

He waited, thinking that Frieta must be slow in coming. His own conscience hardly bothered him. A girl was a girl to him. Mother or daughter, what was the difference? He wasn't married to either of them. A man had to take what he could get, now days.

Alice looked at him, then shifted over snugly against him. "Frieta ain't comin', honey," she informed him, tenderly. She was as blind as ever to her daughter and the man's sensual affair. Not once did she suspect that he could be wanting her daughter instead of her.

"Why isn't she comin'?" he asked, giving her a hard, inquisitive stare.

"We had a fallin' out. I struck her. So just drive off and leave her here."

He started the car, drove on down Kansas Avenue.

"What's goin' on between you two?" he asked. He thought for a moment that it might have been what he wanted to tell her. Then he decided that it wasn't. Alice was acting too gentle, too self-composed in his company.

"She's all dolled up," Alice said. "She's makin' a go for that Charley Boyles, I guess. At least that's what she told me. He give her enough dough to start a small bank, from the way she's gone on a buyin' spree."

Eddie nodded, but did not respond. He was contemplating the affair between the daughter and mother. It did not bother him too much. He didn't really give a damn. Certainly he did not intend to marry Alice or her daughter. He only pleasured them for his own kicks. After them there would be others. Still he was very fond of Frieta. She was something special, real nice, damn good!

"Hey, where've you been?" Alice wanted to know. "I haven't seen you for three days or more. Don't you know we're engaged, or had you forgotten that you proposed to me and give me a ring to wear?"

He grinned at her. His dark, deceiving eyes roved over her open collar, the pink blouse she wore disturbed him. Made him think of Frieta. He longed for the tenderness of Frieta's kisses again.

"Gamblin', babe," he said. "Can't just idle round. Can't do that. Makes me jumpy. I'd think of killin' myself. I'm th' nervous type of monkey who can't stand bein' a sittin' duck. Where you wanna go for a ride?"

"I don't want to go for no ride," she said. "You ought to know where I want to go. Or do you?" She placed a hand on his flank nearest her, and caressed him tenderly.

He looked down at her and nodded. He knew very well what she wanted with him. Alice was oversexed, and she did not hesitate to let herself go begging when she was starved.

"I've got some liquor in the back seat," he said. "Three fifths. That ought to be plenty."

"That's too damn much," she said. "I've got to go to work tomorrow. I don't want to go on a damn drunk, honey. Frieta's outa my hands now."

He nodded but did not speak. He was contemplating a scheme to drown her out, fix the pleasure for Frieta and himself for a while. He knew Alice was a sop, a complete dipsomaniac when the drinks were placed before her. He would fix her good and proper. He didn't give a damn. Maybe he'd give her enough to kill her. Then he would be free to have Frieta anytime he chose. The kid was weak for him, crazy, a dope. She was young and green. He would have a dinner with her every day. What a pair of hot-fish he had found on his line.

They crossed the stateline into the Missouri side, and Eddie started looking around on Main street for a cheap hotel to take her to.

"Say, where'd you get money to buy this rattletrap?" Alice questioned him.

"Dice was loaded," he grinned. "I hit and hit, so I win myself a car. How's that?"

"I didn't reckon you stole it," she remarked dryly. "When we gonna get married, Eddie? Or are we?"

"Sure, I reckon," he said. He did not wish to discuss marrying her any longer. It was a sickening thought, now that he had tasted Frieta. Maybe if he was to prolong her, she would become disgusted and break her own engagement, realizing that he had been lying to her all along.

"You sure don't tell me anythin', do you?" she said suspenseful-like. "I don't think you love me like you used to. Do you?"

"Of course, Alice. I'm tryin' to see myself hooked and tryin' to live true to you. After all, that's th' only way marriage has to work."

"Well, you're th' one who proposed, I didn't."

"Can't you give a guy time to think how he's gonna manage?"

"I don't wanna be dead and buried before you make up your mind," she said. She wanted to mention about his arrests which McShane had told her about, but she dare not. She didn't want him to get nervous, or angry with her.

"How much this car cost you?" she asked, as he applied the breaks, stopping before the Hotel Muzzo on Main street.

"Five-hundred bucks," he answered.

"By the way, just how much did you win, gambling?"

"A thousand or so." He looked at her as if he felt she was trying to place a clinch on him and the money which had been given to Frieta. "Why?" he asked.

"You never offered me nothin'," she said. "I'm broke. I need some dough. We're engaged, aren't we."

"I'll give you a hundred bucks when we get inside the hotel," he told her. "That okay, Alice?"

"Suits me," she giggled, climbing out the car. When they were together on the sidewalk, she caught his arm and hurried inside the hotel.

The hotel lobby was no more than ten by twenty feet, with a two-by-four desk just to the left of the stairway. There wasn't a chair or lounge in the small remaining space before the desk. An old man sat behind the desk, and the moment he looked up and saw them before the counter he knew why they had come for a room.

Eddie paid the room rent for one night, but cautioned the old man that he might stay a couple more nights if the young lady persisted. Alice giggled, but hurried up the stairs with her lover.

When they were inside the room, Eddie locked the door, then carried the package of liquor, which he had brought along, to the dresser. Alice crossed over to the window and drew the blinds. The room was dusky dark, and they didn't need to turn on a light.

In some other room down the hall a radio was playing. Alice turned back to the bed and started snapping her fingers and humming the tune to herself. She pulled back the sheet and spread, while Eddie stood at the dresser opening one of the fifths of liquor.

Alice didn't need to be coaxed. She knew why they were there, and she certainly knew what she needed. Her sensual starvation made her nearly desperate, and she could hardly wait for him to feed her, relieve her savage appetite.

She dropped down on the bed and kicked off both her slippers. As Eddie turned with a glass and the liquor bottle, she was standing beside the bed pulling her skirt down and unfastening her blouse.

"Did I tell you I wanted a drink first?" she smiled sweetly.

"Don't you?"

"Wait until we get in bed. I want to rest a while. I don't want to get drunk, I said. I've had some toddies already, and I'm hopin' to go to work in the mornin'."

He placed the whiskies on the table by the bed, and as she unfastened her brassiere, she found his arms round her, fondling her, pawing her thrusting nipples. An uncontrollable desire besieged him. The madness intensified as his lips found hers. He was so brutal until she shoved him away.

"Take it easy, honey," she said, breathlessly. "You'll crush the breath outa me."

He dropped his hands, and his breath, which had mounted, deceased again. He stepped back and flung off his jacket, tore a woolen jersey over his head and watched her standing naked before him. He dropped his trousers, unfastened his shorts. He was a massive man, and Alice realized what she would miss if she didn't get him for her bedmate permanently. His slender frame bulged near the shoulders, and he could have been a young Tarzan.

"My, you're handsome, Eddie," Alice sighed. "Come here and let me feel you. Oh, gee, oh, my!"

As he crossed over to her she saw his flesh. Her lips parted. Her eyes blinked with a mad lust which she had never felt before.

When he was beside the bed, she caught him round the hips, gingerly caressed him.

"Oh, how I need it," she crooned, as she fell over on the bed and he came upon her.

For a moment he kissed her tenderly, and then the madness developed in him again. Alice clung to him desperately, knowing that she would be really satisfied this evening, above all others. It looked to her as if Eddie had been conserving himself especially for her.

"My head's been killin' me," she said. "I've had nasty dreams. I'm crazy I guess. I can't do without it. Not yet, honey. Not yet."

He was kissing her throat, then both breasts, and his lips moved down to her stomach. She intwined her fingers in his hair, and felt herself growing emotional, fierce for his contact.

Her left hand crawled down past his stomach and she massaged him until he was kissing her madly.

"Not yet," she murmured, wanting to prolong the sweetness, the savage bliss.

He rolled her over on her back and moved between her.

"Give, babe. Give," he moaned anxiously.

Her fingers clawed, her lips parted. Her teeth clamped on one shoulder and held tight.

Alice shuddered as she felt the sudden sweetness of his contact. Her lower self burned and sloshed from his friction. Her legs hung gradually free from him, then as the thrill gripped her soul, her flanks reached desperately after the ceiling.

He was more primitive than ever this evening. He was a demon, and she found herself plunged wildly into a chasm of bliss which made rivulets of sweat pour from her body. Her skin was flushed with waves of dimpled sweat bubbles like blood on her raging flesh. She plunged on and on, wilder and breathless into a gratification of heathenly sensation.

At last she uttered a harsh outcry of delight and breathless passion, then flung herself outwards, gasping for breath, and completely satisfied. She relaxed with closed eyes, smiling inwardly of the pleasant aftermath of sexual gratification.

CHAPTER SIX

H E BROUGHT HER A DRINK when she had recuperated. Alice sat upon the bed and reached for his lips with hers as he handed her a glass of whisky. She knew she had not had enough, not just one time. Today she was more insatiable than ever. Her body screamed to be crushed until she could hardly walk. She dreamed it, crazed for it. It was compulsory.

"Do I satisfy you, honey?" she crooned, before taking a swallow of liquor. "Do I make you feel good?"

He stood by the bed drinking from the bottle. "Any man would lose his mind if he just saw you naked one moment, Alice," he flattered her. "Want another drink?"

She nodded, having finished that one.

"I can't understand what's wrong with me, Eddie," she giggled. "I just want you and want you and want you. I'm nothin' but a goddamned pig, I guess. But you know, it's th' truth. Honey, you're just like this glass of booze; the more one tastes of you, the more she wants you. How many gals have you ever had tell you that?"

"You're th' first one, Alice."

"You're a liar. You don't have to hand me that line. Come sit on the bed with me. Pour me some more whisky. This one's gone, too."

He stepped forward and poured her another glass of liquor. She swallowed it with one quick thrust of the glass to her lips. Then she settled back on the bed, holding out her arms to him as he crawled back in the bed with her.

"Care to pester me some more right now?" she asked anxiously. "I feel it real bad again."

"We should see more of each other," he grinned, lifting her legs and crawling between them again.

"You know where I live, honey," she said. "Frieta knows 'bout me. She's no baby. Oh, damn if I can understand what's she's doin' with so much dough, anyhow. I can stand a gal who hustles and admits, but one who comes right before my face and tells a goddamn stinkin' lie ought to be beat to death. If she's got some guy old enough for her old man givin' her dough, why don't she come right out and say so. I wouldn't mind. She's old enough to git married. Frieta's old 'nough to sleep with a man. I want her to. I wouldn't want her to go along livin', destroying herself if she wants to do it. I'd bet she's got somethin' right nice on her. Do you suppose?"

He was insinuating himself between her. She undulated her hips slowly, gritting her teeth as the pleasure surged through her body.

"Frieta is beautiful," he said. He didn't know why he said it. "She's real nice."

"You don't have to tell me. I can look at her hips and her rear and see that she's been doin' it before now. Any woman knows what the other does when she starts swelling out. You ever notice Frieta's breasts. Ain't they thick. Sonsofbitchin' school chums work. They feelin' her somethin' awful. She's easy. Goddamn her. I hope she'll learn some sense before it's over. I can't see her takin' patterns after me, Eddie. Oh, baby, that feels so good!"

In a little while they were shivering and pumping themselves at each other again. It came quicker this time. Alice caught his shoulders, braced her thighs up and let him take her very hard before she fell back in despair, but it was such a sensual despair of ecstasy.

"Pour me another drink," she sighed from the bed.

Eddie was too glad to oblige her. He brought a fifth over to the bed. She sat up, her back resting against the bedstead.

She leaned and caressed his broad shoulders, rubbed her tousled hair against the side of his left cheek.

"Baby, you're so sweet," she said. "Oh, I'll just die if you ever left me. I would, Eddie. Pour me 'nother drink. I said I wasn't gonna git drunk, but who cares....who in hell cares if I do. Do you, Baby? Huh?"

"Take it easy, Alice," he said. He made sure that he drank only mildly, but he was feeding the liquor to her in great quantities. Alice failed to notice his tricky scheme. She was blind, only to her insatiated desire for him.

"You ought to make me stop drinkin'," she giggled at him, one hand resting on his shoulder. "I've got to go to work, I told you. Make me stop, Eddie. Please."

"You know you don't wanna stop," he grinned. "Here, have another. Do you or don't you?"

"Pour me 'nother drink, you sop head. Go on...pour.... pour! Don't slight me, baby. After I kill this one I want some more of that other from you. Can I depend on it or not? You too petered out?"

"We need to see more of each other, sugar," he grinned. "Hand me your glass and we'll see."

She finished the drink and handed him the glass. As he rose from the bed to place the liquor on the chest she settled herself in the middle of the bed a third time, parted herself and reached out her blond arms for him as he crawled back to her again.

By now Alice was nearly dizzy, and she could feel the liquor working on her. It was no doubt that she would be completely drunk in a few more hours.

As he insinuated himself against her, he felt all the energy leave her body. She did not respond with the alacrity which she had earlier. He imagined she was just about spent, and this was only because she was working on impulse and a savage greediness for sexual stimulant.

Before the complete fulfullment had been attained, Alice fell out on him. She was snoring drunkardly in the next hour. He lay idle beside her for some while, and then fell asleep also.

Some while, after darkness, Eddie rose from the bed and dressed. He was slightly dizzy, but not in such a state of drunkenness that he was completely unaware of reality. He turned on a light and looked at Alice. She lay on her back, her arms thrown to both sides, her thighs flung outwards. He marveled the sight of her pinkish naked body, but he dreaded the beastly drunkardly manner in which she snored. Her hair lay tousled, wildishly about her head, and her lips hung open in a beastly snarl, and as if the fierce madness of desire still possessed her slumber, her drunken slumber. Her flesh had a curious sweat-perfumed odor.

Eddie grinned at her, then turned to the liquor on the dresser. He observed that they had consumed a fifth and a half. A bottle and one half of a bottle was left. This would not be enough to hold Alice. He wanted her to stay there as long as her whisky would hold out. He didn't care if she died there. He wanted Frieta. With Alice out of his way, he would have straight access to her pretty hot-natured daughter.

He stepped to the phone and called the desk, telling the old clerk to have the porter bring up three more fifths of liquor. He didn't have any preference, any kind would be satisfactory.

Eddie sat on the side of the bed smoking. He waited for the boy with the liquor. As his dark eyes rested on Alice's despondently savage position, a heated madness seized him, and he had a fierce desire to spend the entire night with her, and forget about her daughter. What if Frieta had changed her mind about him after she and Alice had fallen out over the money? Maybe she'd fear him now, or grown cold to his caresses in fear of retaliation of her mother's accusations. Girls were like that. They changed their minds quicker than the weather. One moment they felt themselves crazily in love, the next moment they were only pretending and didn't love you after all.

A light rap on the door brought Eddie out of his dazed stupor. He rose and went across the room to the door. When he opened the door the porter, wearing a blue uniform, handed him a brown paper sack with three fifths of liquor. Eddie took the sack and carried it over to the dresser. Returning to the door, he extracted twenty-dollars from his pants pocket and gave it to the porter, telling him to keep the change. The man thanked him and turned away. Eddie shut the door and turned back to the dresser and the whisky. He took all three of the fifths out of the sack and lined them across the dresser so Alice wouldn't fail to see them when she awakened. She would be mad for a drink when she came to. He would not be there, but she must be able to help herself. He didn't wish to marry her, now. He had changed his mind, and this was his answer to her constant demands on the subject.

Carefully, Eddie tore off the seals of two of the fifths, and the third he opened completely. There were four and a half fifths of whisky for Alice to absorb. Whether she would actually fall for his dirty trick, was yet to be seen. Tonight, he was positive she would not come to. Maybe by the following morning, she would. Then she would be craving another drink, and all day tomorrow. She was the weakened type who could not resist once the temptation had seized her. He was positive he would be able to spend, at least, three whole nights and days with Frieta before Alice sobered. And he hoped she never sobered.

Turning from the dresser he staggered over to the bed and looked down at her. His right hand went between her, and he fingered her a moment in order to make sure she was dead drunk. She was all right. If she hadn't been, his finger would have caused her to stir immediately.

He stopped and kissed her lips, in his mind, wishing her a happy drunk spell. Then he turned towards the door, opened it and left the room, leaving the light burning.

Upon reaching the downstairs lobby, Eddie paused at the desk. The porter was on by this time. The elderly gentleman left. It was nearly ten P.M.

He paid the room rent for three more days and told the boy should the girl in that particular room inquire for him, to inform her that he'd be back shortly. In this way he knew Alice would wait for him, despite how long it would take. She was foolishly in love with him, and he felt himself master to a complete idiot as Alice Ingram.

The porter said that he would carry out his orders, and Eddie left him another five-dollar tip in order to convince him. The porter grinned and nodded his approval of the money.

Once in the Ford, Eddie wasted no time driving back to Kansas and on to Kansas avenue to the apartment where he hoped to find Frieta.

He parked the car in the next block, climbed out and locked it. Then he turned on his heels and returned to the apartment.

He opened the hallway door and made sure that it didn't slam. He didn't want the old lady who lived across the hallway from the Ingrams to hear him. She might become suspicious, and could cause him a great deal of trouble.

Cautiously Eddie mounted the stairs. Several of the old wooden steps squeaked, and he fought to lighten his weight.

Upon reaching the room door, he found the door key which Alice had given to him some while back. He unlocked the door and entered the apartment. He shut the door carefully, hoping that Frieta didn't take him for a rapist, or a robber. In that case he'd have to stand the consequences.

The rooms were warm. He heard the furnace humming. It was January in June, he thought.

He heard no sounds. In the darkness he could not be sure whether Frieta's bedroom door was open or not. Anyway, he'd have to take that gamble. Already he felt himself becoming warm for the feel of her sensual flesh. Her kisses put added power into his manhood. He was inspired into mounting visions as he pulled off his jacket and unfastened his trousers. In his shorts he groped his way towards her bedroom in the darkness, nervously suspenseful to his disappointment if Frieta would repulse him.

His grimy fingers clutched the doorknob, and the door squeaked open. He shut the door silently. Motionless, he listened intently. Then he was justified. She was in the bed all right. Her audible snores reached him. He grinned to himself, thinking how surprised she would be to feel him beside her all night. What a sweet heaven this was going to be, what a paradise of sweetness for the next few days with this tenderly sexy girl, who he felt wanted him as much as he wanted her. He had not given her a thousand dollars for just one moment of sensual love. He felt that she belonged to him. He owned her; she had been bought. She was just as much a prostitute as any who he'd find hustling along the Avenue.

Slowly he tiptoed over to the bed, removing his shoes. He leaned down and pulled back the cover and crawled in the bed. Frieta had not stirred.

As his arms went around her body, feeling her warm buttocks and hips pressing against him, she came to life.

Screaming, Frieta fought her way free of him, thinking he was an intruder, a rapist. She screamed a second time. She leaped up, but he jerked her back in the bed and clamped his hand over her mouth.

"Goddamn you," he cautioned. "It's me, Eddie! Hush up . . . . hush up!"

His voice was enough to confidence her that he wasn't any attacker. Gasping for her breath, she settled back against the wall, staring across at his looming form in the darkness.

"Heavens, Eddie," she moaned breathlessly, "don't scare me like that any more. Where's mama?"

"I left her in Missouri," he said. "Do I have to remind you that I'm crazy 'bout yuh babe?"

She wasn't satisfied with just this slight explanation. "Where did you leave her in Missouri?"

"Come on, kid. She's okay. She's asleep. Don't upset ya'self any more. Alice ask me to come over to see 'bout you. She's drunk, and didn't care t'come back to the apartment in her condition."

"Eddie, you're real dirty," she accused. "You're rotten and no good. You get right out of here ....go on, get out of my room or I'll scream!"

He was angry then. She was ordering him around. This would never do. Somehow he felt that this would happen. She had his money, now she was finished with him. One little effort from her with her kicks and she didn't care to be bothered with him any more.

"I gave you a thousand bucks, babe," he said. "Wasn't that 'nough?"

"You don't own me for it. I never sold out to you. Now, just get outa my room, before I scream for Gladys."

"Do I have to knock some sense in you?"

"You'd better not lay a hand on me."

"I'll half kill you if you make one sound. Now come on and lay down here with me. Don't keep shovin' me 'round, kiddo."

"You're engaged to Alice. You're mama's boy friend. Not mine. I don't want you. You're no good. You're dirty."

"Want me to tell Alice all 'bout us?"

"You'd better not."

"Then come on and give me some."

"No . . no. I'm not doing anything with you any more. I was crazy that day. I didn't have good sense. I was crazy...I tell you...real, batty...real gone nuts! Oh, I hate myself...I hate myself for doing what I did with you for all that money. Alice won't ever forgive me, her own daughter with her man. Get out … get outa my room, Eddie LaRose!"

He cursed, and lunged across the bed. She tried to dodge him, but he caught her off guard. She struggled as he caught her arms and hurled her down against the bed. Beating against his face, she squirmed and grunted, straining every ounce of strength in her body to fight him off. But he was too powerful, and he easily pinioned her down on the bed.

Thrusting her apart, he flung himself between and took her viciously, while she whined and made slight efforts to resist him. Her efforts soon dwindled to nothing, and she found herself mounting into a reality of bliss beyond her own dreading pleasures.

"Oh, stop … Eddie. Please, I'll be nice. I'll act nice. Just don't hurt me so bad. Please."

"You want me now?"

"Yes, oh, yes."

"You promise not to fight me any more?"

Her arms crawled round his shoulders, and her flanks rose gradually until she was straining to keep herself from screaming out in a sensual bliss.

"You promise not to tell Alice, now?" she asked.

"Not on my life, sugar."

"You just had her, didn't you?"

"Do I smell that lousy?"

"I feel that you have."

"I'm no good, you said."

"You're a dirty sonofabitch, Eddie. I can't resist you somehow. I know mama can't. You're making both of us your women, your tools. Make up your mind. Which one of us do you really want?"

"You said you didn't want me a moment ago?"

"I was lyin'. You know I was. You must think I'm crazy. I am crazy. I'm ashamed of myself for ever falling in love with you. After this is over, please go away from me. If you don't I'm going to run away. I can't stand mama ever knowing this. It'll nearly kill her."

"I'm goin' to keep you, Frieta," he said. "You're mine. I'm goin' to marry you, and take you to California. We'll run away together."

"Really? Would you really take me?"

"Sure. I'll do it. You'll be my wife; we can leave Alice here. She told me tonight she didn't mind if you got married, or even slept with a man. Seems she knows you're highly-sexed, and has to have it."

She burned now. All her fierce resistance of him which she had felt at first had diminished. She was a different person. She was lust and desire, a mad raging female who could not refuse of reject him. Her passions were exalted and inflamed. The fierceness of her quickened hips made her insane and nearly senseless.

"I want you, Eddie," she murmured. "But I'm scared of myself. Times I feel crazy....real crazy...you know I think I'm a nymphomaniac...I am...God knows I am!"

He did not answer, but he realized that she was nothing short of a sex maniac. She could not possibly resist a lover, once her body had been touched.

Eddie's hands went beneath Frieta's hips and lifted them. Madly Frieta yielded. She did not seem to care what happened to her any more just as long as she could feel the pressing feeling of release mounting and so murderously pleasurable. Eddie's cheeks were resting between her thighs. The sky seemed to crumble and was suddenly falling down upon her. She winced, and whined and sighed.

"Oh, that...that's sweet...so sweet," she rasped in a strange tone. She clenched her teeth hardly able to bear the mounting pleasure.

Her fingers ripped at Eddie's hair. His lips and tongue showered kisses on her until she was kicking and fighting in a rage unparallel to her own reality. Sparks of pleasure leaped from her loins, again and again. Until she could no longer stop or hold herself, she shouted like a squealing pig and fell back exhaustedly upon the bed.

CHAPTER SEVEN

THE FOLLOWING MORNING it started raining again. The wind blew and a fury not much short of a hurricane was released against the area. Within a matter of a few minutes the streets were young streams, since the street sewerage would not carry off the excess water fast enough.

At the Muzzo Hotel Alice stirred on the bed. Then she rolled over and called Eddie. Not completely sure where she was or what had happened during the course of the last day, she sat slowly upwards in bed.

Drunkenly, she looked round the room. The light was burning. The dresser was piled with bottles of liquor.

"Eddie!" she moaned in a husky tone. "Eddie, you in th' bathroom?"

Weakly she dropped back down on the bed and gave a low curse. Then she summoned enough strength to roll herself over to the edge of the bed. She climbed off the bed to the floor, staggered over to the dresser. There, she paused, lifted a bottle of liquor and took a long pull at it. With a tired blow, she twisted her head and looked round the corner of the room until she could see inside the bathroom. No one was in there.

"Wonder where he went?" she sighed drunkenly. "I told him I never wanted to git mahself drunk."

She raised the bottle again to her lips and took another drink. Her thirst was somewhat abated. So she staggered over to the window and made a clumsy effort to pull back the blinds. The rain was pouring down, and obscure gloomy weather hung over the area. She could not imagine what time of day it was or even what day it was, nor how long she had been there. She didn't seem to care. All she wanted was Eddie. But he wasn't there. She did not sense that he could have stepped out. She was not as drunk as she had been the past night.

Alice turned away from the window and crossed the room to the phone. She clutched the phone, taking it from the hook. The clerk answered. She inquired if her boy friend had gone out. The clerk stated that he'd left word that he would be right back. That satisfied Alice. So she dropped the receiver, then wobbled back to the bed and sat down. She took another drink, and still another. Then as if she could not resist the temptation, she turned up the bottle and drained it.

Conscious of the empty bottle, she let it drop to the floor, then she curled back upon the bed and fell off to a drunkenly sleep again.

In the afternoon, Alice awakened. She looked round, hoping to see her lover in the bed. She called him again. That was the only thing she could think of or say by now. She kept repeating his name, unable to think or reason.

She managed to get out of the bed. She staggered across the room until she was in the bathroom. Vaguely she was able to sit on the stool. The pressing release of her excess made no impression on her. Then she rose and reentered the bedroom. Still she could hear the rain dripping from the old hotel eaves. She went to the dresser and selected another fifth of whisky. Back on the bed she took a drink, then dropped the bottle and the liquor gurgled out on the bed around her nude body. Alice fell into a drunken sleep again.

The maid came to the room, unlocked the door and looked in at the drunkard woman sprawled on the bed. Then she turned her nose and closed the door. The strong odor of intoxicants repulsed her. She would not have to be bothered with doing that room this particular day.

All night Alice did not stir, not until late the following day. And it was the maid who entered the room to see about her. She removed all the excess whisky, which Alice had not yet touched. Then she went to the bed and shook Alice.

Alice opened her eyes and looked groggily up at the woman. Her voice was dry and husky.

"How'dy, baby," she said. "Get me a drink, will yuh?"

"Honey, you'd better not drink any more," the maid advised her. "I threw all that whisky away. You'll be sick if you don't stop drinkin'."

"Now, what'd you go and do that for?" Alice winced. "I need a drink. Just one little one." She raised her left fingers, reaching for the maid to help her.

"Get up," said the maid. "You've got yourself in a mess. Look at that filthy sheet and bed."

The maid helped her over to a chair and Alice fell into it She watched groggily as the maid changed the bed.

"Have you seen my man?" Alice asked her, as the maid pulled the filthy sheet from the bed and hauled it over against the door to be taken from the room. "He was here with me. Where'd Eddie go?"

"He's gone, honey. He's deserted you."

"You're kiddin'."

"I wish I was."

"Eddie wouldn't do me that dirty."

"I wish I could agree with you." The maid shook her head disgustedly at the sodden mattress. She turned it over and continued to make up the bed with fresh linen.

"You gonna help me sober up?" Alice asked her. "Will you, please?"

"Sure I will. What can I do for you?"

"Get me somethin'. You know, somethin' to help me sober up. Mah head's hurtin'. I sure would like a drink. Can't you just accommodate me this once?"

"Honey, lie back down, and I'll see what I can do for you."

Alice pulled herself out of the chair, staggered back to the bed and dropped back down. No sooner was she back on the bed, she had fallen into a drunken rest again.

The maid shook her head disgustedly, gathered up all the dirty linen and left the room.

For the next ten hours, Alice found no respite from her ailment. Only the following morning she awakened to find herself again near normal, since she had not had any liquor for the past twenty hours. She had sobered.

Climbing out of the bed, she crossed the room to the dresser and looked hard at her broken features. Her hair was in shambles, her eyes sottish brownishly stained from drinking, her cheeks were hollow, being without food all that time. She was very sick and undernourished. For the first time since she had started the drinking spree with Eddie LaRose, she felt that he had deserted her, left her alone in the room with enough liquor to kill herself. There wasn't a dime on the dresser for her to get a bite to eat. He had lied to her, tricked her. She was a fool to have trusted the dirty bastard, she thought. All he wanted from her were his kicks. How right McShane had been. The scoundrel ought to be hung, beaten until he bled to death.

Crushed and heartbroken that Eddie would treat her so cruelly, Alice covered her face and sobbed. Her features melted in her tears, and she felt as though she wanted to die.

Realizing that tears would not mend her broken spirits, she went into the bathroom and ran water to take a bath. She cried all the while she was in the tub, and even when she washed her face and had returned to the room to powder and apply lipstick. While combing her hair she felt nauseated, so she ran into the bathroom and puked. She heaved again and again. After she had relieved herself, she felt much better. Only she still had the hangover. She was ready to go back to the apartment, to Frieta.

While she dressed slowly, she thought about the money which Frieta had. How foolishly ignorant she was not to have suspected all along that Eddie must have been making a try for her daughter. She did not know for sure, but she could not imagine him treating her so horribly unless there was another woman whom he wanted to be with. If it had been some other woman, why on earth didn't he just tell her so. Yet he hadn't. He had tried to murder her, making her commit suicide by drinking herself to death. That had been his ambition. Why? Was he really the one who had given Frieta all the money? Eddie had told her he had won over a thousand dollars gambling. Certainly all this didn't make sense. What was the sonofabitch after? She thought.

As she left the room she realized that she was definitely finished with Eddie. She was going to throw the engagement ring in his face and tell him to go to hell. Funny, how she didn't have enough sense to listen to McShane when he had tried to advise her about the rascal. Eddie had promised her a hundred dollars. Not one penny had he given her, not even for the shellacking she had given him. She was so extremely disgusted and angry at Eddie LaRose until she felt like taking a revolver and killing him. If she just didn't love him so much, she could believe that something must have pulled him away from her.

Downstairs in the lobby, Alice stopped at the desk to inquire about her lover.

The old man looked up at her as she paused before him. He knew very well that the man who had come with her had left her drunk there and deserted her. He forced a silly grin as he reflected over the facts.

"Good mornin'," Alice said. She cast a glimpse outside. It was still raining.

"How'dy, ma'am," the old man spoke quietly. "Still nasty weather, we havin'." He went on.

"So I see," Alice replied. "What time is it?"

He turned and looked at a big black-faced electric clock behind the desk.

"Ten A.M.," he said, facing her again.

"How many days have I been in this dump?"

"Well, let's see. 'bout three, I'd reckon. Let me see my book." He fumbled with a long gray ledger book under a shelf on the counter. He ruffled some pages, then looked slowly up at her. "Yep. Three days. You came here on Tuesday evenin'."

"It's Friday, huh?" she asked.

"That's correct, ma'am," he grinned.

She looked into his eyes, thinking that at his age, which looked to be seventy or more, he ought to be truthful.

"Do you remember the guy who came here with me?" she asked.

"Yes, ma'am. I sure do."

"When was the last time you saw him here with me?"

"Why, that dude never even stayed the night with yuh, so th' boy said when I come down the next mornin'."

"That means he checked out Tuesday night, doesn't it?"

The old man nodded.

"Do I owe you anything?" she asked.

"Nope. Your rents been paid up until today."

"Why, the dirty sonofabitch!" she swore. "Wait'll I get my hands on him. Do you see how dirty he done me? We're supposed to be engaged, too!"

"I wouldn't have guessed it."

"Brother, we're not, any more!" She looked at him a moment, fighting back tears. "Do me a favor, please. Call me a taxi."

He nodded and put the call through for the cab.

Alice ordered the taxi driver to take her back to Kansas to Smiley's tavern. It was pay day. She could at least get her money, but she doubted if she had a job. Smiley didn't take any such foolishness as his waitresses staying off the job and returning whenever they felt like it. The help were required to call if sick. She hadn't called, so she would be fired.

Unfortunately, she was right. She was fired. As she alighted from the cab and entered the tavern, she spied a tall red haired girl with freckles behind the bar for the morning shift, which was the shift she had worked. The red head told her that Smiley wasn't in, but the cook wanted to see her. In the kitchen, the cook gave her her pay envelope, telling her that Smiley couldn't use her any more. Alice thanked him and left.

Outside, she was about to pay off the taxi driver when Duke Wayne drove up in a new black Buick. He honked the horn at Alice and she ran over to the car just as he opened the door.

"Well, hello, sugar," Duke grinned at her. "You off so early?"

"I'm fired. I don't work at Smiley's any more, honey."

"What's th' matter with you? You look sick. Been drinkin'?"

"You said it. Do I look that lousy?"

"Honest, sugar."

"I'm goin' home and eat somethin'. I haven't tasted a bit for three days. It's a wonder I'm still alive. That goddamn bum who I was engaged to, left me in a hotel room to drink myself to death. Wasn't that dirty?"

"I can't believe it."

"Well, it's true. He wanted to murder me. Why? You're a cop. Why would a guy treat a gal so dirty? Bein' engaged, too."

He frowned angrily. His temper was intensified, upon hearing such hideous news.

"I figure he was done with you. That's why. What other reason?"

"That's what I figured too. Funny, how dumb some gals are when they've had a guy once or twice. He's all they want and need to satisfy them. Then he isn't what they figured, after all." She looked back at the taxi who was waiting for her to pay him. "I owe this cabman. Wait, honey. You gonna drive me home?"

"I sure am. And you just sit tight, Alice. I'll pay the taxi for you. You're real sick. Your eyes are deceiving, if you're not."

"Thanks, Mr. Wayne."

Duke climbed out the car and went back to pay off the taxi driver, while Alice leaned back in the car and closed her eyes to hold back her miserable feeling.

Upon his return to the car, Duke drove off. He told her all about himself. His wife had divorced him six months ago, taken their two children with her. He didn't know where she went, nor had he heard from her. Anyway, he was glad to get rid of her, although he cherished the kids. His wife was completely cold towards him, and they found themselves quarreling every day. A separation was the only means to make each of their lives better.

He told her that he was looking for a nice girl who wanted to make a decent home, and one who wasn't always too afraid she was going to become pregnant every time it happened. His wife had been allergic to sexual gratification, and he could no longer withstand her cold indifferent nature towards the one joy on earth which he found so greatly appetizing.

Alice studied him in a different sense, now. Why hadn't she given him her address earlier. Perhaps all this silly affair with Eddie LaRose could have been avoided. She felt the same way about life as he felt. They were identical, and should make a nice loving couple. She could easily break herself from drinking with the right man to pleasure her every night.

When they reached the apartment she invited him up to the rooms. He took a seat on the divan, while she made some coffee, and saw to it that she had some hot soup to give her body nourishment. Frieta wasn't home, and Alice felt that she would be taking her singing lessons, this being Friday.

Duke was very interesting. He had a hard serious voice, and he was as handsome as sin. He wanted to come to see her, if she decided to break her engagement, and she promised him that he could start right then, for it was already broken.

Alice sat down beside him and he placed his arms about her, snuggling her body close against his. She assumed that he must be starved for love, being separated from his wife all that time. She meant to see if he would be true to her, before she spent any more time with any man. Yet she knew she was weak when the thirst came upon her. It would bother her as soon as she had regained her stamina. She knew that as well as she was seated on the divan.

When Duke was ready to leave, he kissed her at the door. Alice felt her stomach quiver, wishing he had been the one who had occupied her time for the past week instead of Eddie LaRose.

When Duke had left her, she dropped down on the divan and cried harder. But she swore the moment she saw Eddie LaRose she was going to try to kill him!

CHAPTER EIGHT

EDDIE LAROSE WAS SEATED AT A BAR on lower Kansas avenue. It was close to eight P.M. He had spent three sex-filled mornings and nights with Frieta Ingram, and he now felt that the girl was a raging beast and he didn't think he could possibly extinguish her sexual-greediness. Frieta was an uncivilized nymphomaniac, boldly engrossed with a female madness which he had never found in a girl before.

As he nursed a rum and soda, he thought about Alice. She was very sexed, but not half as desperate as her young daughter. The first night Frieta had been warm, but the next morning she had thrown herself at him with a crazed velocity which had sapped the strength from his body as if he was helpless. He had left during the day, for fear the old woman across the hallway would come in on them, but he had returned during the night to taste Frieta again and again. She never seemed to be satisfied. Her hunger for passion was insatiable.

Each morning he had phoned the Muzzo Hotel to inquire about Alice, mostly to make sure she was still there, and whether she was alive or dead. Each time he had called the old hotel clerk had informed him that she was there, drunk in the room. The third morning which was Friday, she had checked out. Alice would be back at the apartment that particular night and he dare not show up to be with Frieta, even though his lust was greatly overwhelming enough.

The tavern was very crowded, but Eddie was too preoccupied with his own thoughts to notice the other drinkers around him.

Some way he must eliminate Alice for good. It was impossible for Frieta to tell her about their affair, and Alice would probably want to murder him for his disloyalty. Whatever, he must face the consequences. He could not possibly lose Frieta, now, knowing her for what she was. She was a man's delight, his greatest desire. She was a jewel in her sexual desires.

That particular morning he had driven Frieta out in the country, along a deserted road, near the Kaw River. They had talked about plans to elope, but Frieta did not feel entirely certain that she wanted to do it immediately. She had to tell Alice how she felt about herself, so her mother would understand. Never before had she realized that she possessed such a morbid sickness until she had given herself to Eddie. Still she had always sex gratified herself into heated passions beyond her own uncivil senses. Frieta felt frightened for herself, but it was such a sweet nervousness when she was with a man. If she fell so easily for Eddie, she would fall easily enough for other boys and men, until she would find herself in a low state which she could never endure.

Eddie finished his drink and left the tavern.

Once he was in the Ford, he drove along slowly on Kansas Avenue, until he had reached the apartment. He thought about going to his own room on Eighteenth for once and going to bed, but he had a taste for love again. Frieta stirred his soul. And then he felt that he might as well face Alice and get everything over with. Frieta had been deeply distressed about her mother, all the three days which she had been at the hotel. She had tried to coax it out of Eddie which hotel she was in, and even threatened to phone the police if he didn't tell her, but he had not told her, and warned her that if she told the police he would be forced to reveal the entire love affair to Alice when she sobered.

Eddie parked the Ford a block from the girl's apartment, climbed out and walked back towards the entrance. He had a sharp-bladed hunting knife which he carried in the right side door pocket, but he didn't imagine he'd need it at this particular moment. After all, Alice might not be as angry at him as he had assumed. He didn't imagine she had enough sense to get angry at him, she was so greatly impassioned for his love. She had told him in bed that she would die if he ever quit her. She obviously meant it or she wouldn't have said it.

A light mist fell, but there was the threat of rain as usual in June.

Eddie turned into the lower hallway, heard the door whining shut behind him. He tossed a cigarette against the hallway floor and mounted the stairs very carefully and patiently.

When he reached the door, he started to knock, but the impulse was too strong to use his door key. So he extracted his doorkey and opened the door and entered the room.

The radio played softly. A table lamp glowed on top of the T. V., other than that every other room was dark.

Alice was asleep on the divan, outstretched in maroon robe. Her thighs showed where it parted. Two pillows were propped behind her head, and she looked very tired and pale in the face. Her arms were dangling to the sides, the right arm hanging over the divan upon the floor. She snored slightly, unconscious of his presence.

Eddie imagined Frieta wasn't there, and recalled her telling him that she was going to a movie which she had been waiting to see when it came to the Avenue.

He stalked over near Alice, paused patiently to light a cigarette. Smoke seeped from his nostrils as he inhaled the cigarette. He had plenty of time. There was no need to become impatient. He did not think Alice could hurt him. She was much too timid looking to even put up a fight. Even his dirty deed did not bother his conscience. He never worried about his misdeeds. Whatever he did he figured it was to his own interest, and certainly his trick on Alice was. He would repeat it any time in order to be with Frieta. He did not think he even wanted to marry Frieta. He might use her as long as he could, and then discard her. Or wait and make her hustle for him. She was wanting very madly, and rich gentlemen would pay highly to bed such a young hot beauty as Frieta.

His presence obviously awakened Alice from her deep slumber. She rolled to one side and her eyes popped open as though her inner conscience warned her of his presence.

With a sudden movement she was seated upright, a hateful frown upon her brow, darkening her complexion. Her eyes were mean and spiteful, loathing the sight of him.

"Eddie!" she scowled. "You bastard .... you rotten dog!" Her bottom lip twisted into a loathful snarl. "You get outa here!"

He perched one hip upon the table, smoking calmly, hardly moved by her wrathfulness. In fact he smiled down at her as though he knew she was joking. Certainly she didn't mean it. Any girl would be upset and cross if she felt she had been made a fool of.

"Calm down, babe," he said smoothly. "Don't flip your lid, see."

Their eyes met. This moment he was staring harder at her. The grin had left his face. He could see the terrible threat looming in her hateful eyes. No longer did he feel that she was joking. This dame meant business. She was definitely full of murder. Her features were frustrated, bitterly enraged.

Alice removed the engagement ring from her finger. She took careful aim to hurl it into his face. The ring struck his bottom lip and bounced off to the floor. It rolled underneath the table and he made no effort to retrieve it.

"Take your goddamn ring and beat it!" she snarled again, even more adamantly. "We're through. I never want to see the sight of you again. So there!"

Eddie felt that he would have something to say about the viciousness of her tongue. He wasn't near finished with matters yet.

He leaned and mashed out the cigarette in an ashtray on the table. Then he stood and took a few steps in her direction. Before her, he grabbed her by the shoulders and braced her up to him and quickly kissed her lips.

She brutally shoved him away, her right hand darting forward. Before he was completely out of her reach, she made a savage lunge for his face. Her long nails lashed down the center of his face, his eyes, nose and mouth the target. There was great power behind the gesture. Enough power to rip the skin of the forehead and bring blood from his nose and lips.

With a snarlish cry of rage, Eddie stepped back out of her range. He felt the pain, but he had to be certain. Both hands felt on his forehead, his nose and lips. As he drew his hand away, he saw the blood upon his fingers. He cursed, then lunged forward at her.

"Yuh bitch!" he snarled. "You whorin' bitch …. I'll teach yuh somethin'."

He swung a hard right fist to her head, knocking her back upon the divan. There was no pity in the punch. He meant to knock her out, despite how cruel he had treated her all along.

Blood gushed from Alice's nose, and her lips were cut as she fell dazed and stunned. She gritted her teeth, however, and held on to her senses, for she felt that this bastard was out to destroy her once and for all.

She saw him coming towards her again, perhaps to deal more punishment to her already impotent body. As he made a motion to reach for her hair, she flung her body into his legs and he went flying over her and landed on his head upon the floor. She had surprised him, caught him entirely off guard.

As Eddie scrambled to rise, Alice made a lunge for a heavy ashtray upon the table. As she contacted it, she wheeled and hurled it at the man. Eddie rose just in time to catch the heavy crockery against his left cheek. The ashtray struck him solidly, and knocked him sideways into a flawful crouch. A deep gash was cut, and blood poured down his cheek to the floor.

Meanwhile, Alice, gasping breathlessly, wheeled, and made a dash towards her bedroom where she kept a revolver in her bottom dresser drawer.

Eddie sensed that she kept a gun in the room, and he had to stop her before she got her hands on it. By now he was well assured that Alice was not joking.

She had hardly reached the door, when he made a dive for her legs. He tackled her just outside the bedroom door, and she twisted her body round, scratching and beating at his face, her blows not the least ineffective. He caught her hair, jerked her head towards him and smashed her in the face.

Alice screamed. Then she shouted for Gladys. She realized she was no match for such a huge and powerful brute.

Yet she was not potentially feeble. Powerful fingers caught his coat, yanked it over his head, ripped his shirt and he was suddenly blinded. Then she tried to rise, but he caught her legs, ripping off her smock, tearing away her slip and brassiere. Blood gushed from a hideous cut in Eddie's left cheek, where her claws had gouged into his flesh.

Alice managed to tear herself free once more. Though dazed and fighting for breath, she reached her feet. Her eyes set on a table lamp upon the television. It was burning along with the ceiling light. She jerked it from the cord. The lamp went out. Alice wheeled with wild hair, flushed bloody face, and hurled the lamp upon Eddie's head. The glass broke and dispersed about upon his shoulders and body.

"You ain't gonna kill me!" she cried. "Gladys!"

Again she staggered towards the bedroom door, hoping that the lamp would have knocked him cold. But it hadn't. It only helped to intensify his terrible wrath.

As she reached the bedroom door and went through into her bedroom, he was right behind her. Alice snatched at the bottom drawer and missed it. He hurled her away from the dresser. They were between the bed and the cedar chest now. He had her by the hair, yanking her head about in such a horrible manner that she could not think or realize that she existed.

However, Alice screamed pitifully, as he beat her in the face, slammed her head repeatedly against the floor, until she was knocked senseless.

Someone was pounding on the door and calling Alice, now. Breathlessly, Eddie halted his beating the girl. He stood up and staggered to the door and turned on the light in the bedroom. He looked over at Alice's motionless body and didn't know whether she was alive or dead. He was too dizzy himself to even notice her breathing. He heard the old woman across the hallway shouting for Alice.

With a curse, he set his mad eyes across the front room at the hallway door. The old woman was rattling the doorknob, seemingly greatly upset from the manner she pleaded for Alice to open the door for her.

Eddie looked back at Alice's sprawled form. He had a fierce impulse to get a knife from the kitchen and finish her. His murderous eyes measured the distance from where he stood to the kitchen door. The time was short because the old lady had returned to her own quarters and he heard her shouting over the phone for the police.

Eddie made his mind up. He had to beat it. No use of being caught in the act by police.

He staggered over to Alice and started kicking her. He noticed how badly her face was bruised and how it had puffed up from his severe beating. He wanted to break her neck off. Blood from his own face dripped down upon Alice's body. Then Eddie staggered back out the bedroom and crossed over to the door. He opened the door just as Gladys opened her door and spied him coming out.

For a tense moment the old woman and the brutish man eyed one another. He hurled a curse at her and ran down the stairs.

CHAPTER NINE

D<small>R. F</small>ANNY, a thin elderly man with grey hair and a smooth face, finished applying bandages on Alice's battered face and body. It was nearly 10 P.M. now. The little doctor turned to Thomas McShane and Duke Wayne who stood just outside the bedroom door conversing with Gladys Hernden who had given them all the facts as best she could from what she had heard and seen. Immediately after Eddie LaRose had hurried from the building, Gladys had entered to find Alice all bloody and badly mauled lying on the floor. She managed to lift Alice upon the bed and had been washing blood from her face with a wet towel when the two detectives, along with another prowl car of uniformed officers, had arrived. McShane had issued a pick-up order for Eddie LaRose the moment Gladys informed him who Alice's assailant had been.

Dr. Fanny confronted the two detectives. "She's gonna be all right," he said. "No broken bones, only a few bad bruises along her cheeks and bottom lip. She lost one tooth, and one eye has closed. Other than that she'll be all right in a few days. I've given her enough sedatives to keep her quiet for a while, so don't become uneasy if she doesn't wake for some while. I'm drop by tomorrow morning."

The detectives stepped aside for the doctor to pass, and they watched him silently as he went over to Gladys and Frieta who were seated on the divan. He repeated to them what he had said to the others. Frieta was sobbing, holding a white handkerchief over her face. She knew she was to blame for it all, and her conscience was hurting her more than anything else.

Dr. Fanny gathered up his black grip and picked up his hat and coat and left the apartment. Gladys followed him to the door and went out the door with him and closed it.

McShane went over to Frieta and sat down beside her. He had always been fond of the girl. He was more blind as to the facts concerning the situation, since Frieta had told him that she didn't know what it started over.

"Duke tells me that Eddie took Alice to a hotel room and forced whisky on her?" McShane asked.

Frieta removed the handkerchief from her face and studied his odd features.

"I guess he did that," Frieta said.

"Alice was of the opinion that the guy wanted her to drink herself to death?"

"I don't know…. I don't know. She's the one engaged to him, not me!"

"Frieta, I don't know what's goin' on between you and your mother. I don't know who's to blame. Since nobody's been hurt, yet, there's nothin' we can do here. We'll find Eddie LaRose and hold him for battery assault. Meanwhile, you be sure and keep the dirty bastard away from here. He's had over eleven arrests. Served ten years at a Federal Institution at Indianapolis."

"What for?" Frieta wanted to know. This was her first time knowing that. She was beginning to hate the sight of Eddie LaRose, despite her irresistible desire for him.

"Murder!" said McShane. "He was only fifteen when he started his crime wave. If you love your mother, try to help her. Somehow she needs you very badly. Alice is a good girl, she's just had some hard breaks with her boy friends. Some decent chap could easily make her life happier."

Duke was in the bedroom with Alice. He swore that he'd kill the dirty hoodlum if he ever caught him outside the law. He stooped and kissed Alice's puffed lips, then left the room.

McShane was at the front door holding his felt hat when Duke entered the front room. Duke smiled at Frieta.

"From now on, I'm your daddy, baby," Duke informed her. "I like Alice. I like her more than she realizes. I'll be around, Frieta. And don't forget, I'm gonna be your step papa. Savvy?" He winked at her. Frieta smiled uncomfortably, and waved at the two detectives as they left the room and closed the door on her.

A few days later Eddie LaRose was picked up at a pool hall between Eighth and Ninth streets on Central Avenue. He was booked and held without bond for his ruthless assault on Alice Ingram. By now he had spent most of his money which he had won gambling, and therefore, was unable to make bond. So he was held in jail. Neither Alice nor Frieta went to see him, nor did either of them care to. Frieta was just as disgusted and sickened from the looks of the man as Alice was. However, when his trial was held a week later, Alice did not appear. She actually felt that she didn't wish to persecute Eddie, so the man was released, after paying a hundred dollar fine for disturbing the peace.

A week had hardly passed before Alice was stirring round the apartment. She did not have much to say to Frieta, and Frieta thought the reason might have been that she half suspected that Eddie LaRose and her daughter had been having an affair behind her back.

Alice spent a great deal of her time doctoring her bruised complexion. Thus she stayed shut-up in the bedroom more so than ever. She hated her looks. Frieta still possessed five-hundred dollars of money which Eddie LaRose had given her on that horrible, yet heavenly, day when she had first submitted to him. She did not intend to let Alice know that she possessed the money. She feared her mother's reproach on the matter.

And so the days passed slowly. It stopped raining near the first of July. The sun came out and it was very hot again. The furnace was shut off, and the windows to the apartment were raised to let in cooler air.

On the sixth of July, Mike Hernden passed away. Gladys's grievous screams rocked the old apartment building. It happened early in the morning, at four. Alice and Frieta both climbed out of bed and went across to the kitchenette to comfort Gladys, and to help her out in her distress.

The funeral for Mike Hernden was held three days later at a church in the Armourdale district. Gladys's grief was shared by many of her husband's relatives as well as her own. Frieta and Alice attended the funeral, and accompanied the family to the cemetery for the burial.

The following morning after Mike Hernden's funeral, Frieta awakened with a nauseating sick spell. She climbed from the bed and staggered through the front room and dining room towards the bathroom, but was unable to hold it back and spewed up between the living room and the bathroom floor.

Her retchings brought Alice from her bedroom, and she stood at the door looking at Frieta down on her knees emptying her stomach on the carpet.

"What ails yuh, honey?" Alice asked in a sympathetic voice.

Unable to reply, Frieta heaved again, and was finally so exhausted by her constant strains until she fell over on the floor just to the right of the stinking filth.

Alice was naked. She still had a few bandages on her cheeks and her arms. Her eyes were blackened, but the swelling had gone. She staggered back in her bedroom and found a thin wrap. Pulling the wrap round her naked body, she hurried to the girl and lifted her up as much as she could and half carried and pulled her back into her own bedroom, where she put her to bed.

The cramping pains became worst, and Frieta moaned and cried in her misery. Alice hurried to summon Gladys before she began the task of cleaning up the girl's filth.

When Gladys opened the door to Alice's nervous knocks, Alice said,

"Frieta's very sick. Think I should summon Dr. Fanny?"

Gladys still had on her nightgown. It wasn't seven in the morning yet.

"What's ailin' her, Alice?" Gladys asked nervously. "First one thing and then another."

"She's got stomach cramps. Can't you hear her groanin'?"

Indeed Frieta's retching groans sounded quite distinctly throughout the upstairs hallway and the lower part of the old apartment building.

"Let me have a look at her," said Gladys. "Maybe I can tell whether it's only a stomach ache or somethin' else more serious."

"Come on, then," Alice said.

They returned to the bedside, and Gladys pulled down Frieta's sleeping shorties and examined her stomach, and looked into her eyes. Frieta grunted and moaned, staring helplessly up at the two older women.

"Do you have quick pains, baby?" Gladys asked her.

Frieta nodded miserably.

Gladys suspected more than diagnosed the case. But she certainly hit the nail on the head.

After she had studied the matter over, she turned back to Alice and said very softly, somewhat upset herself over what she suspected it to be.

"My sister had eleven kids, honey," Gladys said seriously. "She lived with me in Lexington, Missouri. Every time she got down sick like this, I knew right away, without any doctor's word that she was pregnant. Course, I ain't sayin' your girl's pregnant. It could be just a slight stomach ache, or some other ailment. It sure ain't appendicitis. The pain would be on her lower right side if that was the case. But it sure seems to me she's got what a man gives a woman."

"You really think she's …. ?" Alice's lips parted, and she looked shamefully down at Frieta. It was no doubt that she imagined Frieta was pregnant. She half suspected the girl had her flings. She could tell as sure as daylight that Frieta hadn't been a virgin for many weeks.

Silently, Alice motioned Gladys out of the room, and as they went through the door, Alice reached the doorknob and closed the door on Frieta.

"I'll phone Doc," Alice told her, "and see what he says 'bout her. Why don't you go make some coffee while I clean up this stink she made on my carpet."

Gladys nodded and ambled off into the kitchen to stir up some breakfast for them.

By noon Dr. Fanny had been there and gone. Gladys had left the apartment also, stating she had to go down to the insurance office to see about some business matters on Mike's policies.

Alice was seated in the bedroom with Frieta. Her pains had ceased momentarily, and Frieta was sitting up in bed drinking a glass of orange juice and munching some crispy bacon which Alice had served to her on a tray.

"You feelin' better, now?" Alice asked.

"Much better," Frieta replied. She eyed her mother with a sullen look of suspiciousness, and shame. She, too, guessed what her trouble was. She had definitely witnessed enough pregnant school chums. There had been one-hundred cases of pregnancy the past year during the school term. Quite a number of girl students had dropped from school because of their conditions.

"Did Doc tell yuh what yuh trouble was?" Alice asked her.

Frieta sipped the orange juice, then looked up at Alice. Her answer was a quick shake of her head. But she knew she had lied. Doc had told her.

"If he never told you," said Alice rather crossly, "he sure told me."

Frieta tensed, turned her face towards the window. It was very pleasant outside. The sun was shining and she could hear birds flitting about in a cherry tree next door. Their sweet twitters seemed to instigate her urge to get up.

"Doc said you were knocked up," Alice went on, very harshly. "How many months since your period stopped?"

Frieta turned her face back towards her mother. She had flushed and her eyes were frightened and nervous. "Just one month, Alice," she said.

"Whose baby is it?"

"Do I have to tell you that?"

"Of course you do. Whose ever it is he's gonna marry you, that's why. Now whose is it?"

Frieta dropped her head. Tears formed in her eyes. She bit her lips as all the damnable sense of whose child it was pounced into her memory. She definitely couldn't bring it upon herself to tell Alice the truth. How horrible could she get. How disgraceful. Her own mother's lover. She carried his baby!

"I'm waitin', Frieta," Alice said to her.

Frieta lifted her head and tears were seeping down her pale cheeks.

"I can't tell you. ... I can't ... I can't!" she cried. She looked quickly away.

"Why? You ashamed of the guy? You wasn't ashamed of him when he thrilled you. T'was good, wasn't it? What's to be ashamed of? He had you. You had him. Maybe he don't know you're this way? Don't you reckon he ought to provide for his own baby?"

"Please, Alice ... please!" Frieta moaned. She was in a mental purgatory. "I don't want to talk about it ... please!"

"You may as well tell me, you'll have to anyway before it's done. Why be ashamed of a man who yuh think 'nough of to have a baby for him?"

She looked hard at Alice. Her eyes were nearly blinded with tears.

"It isn't him who I'm ashamed of, Mama. It's myself. I'm so ashamed of myself until I feel like taking my own life!"

Alice studied her very carefully. Then she stood and stepped over to the dresser. She picked up a cigarette and put a glowing match to it. Smoking casually, she turned and looked thoughtfully back at Frieta. Her mind was centered on the dirty trick which Eddie LaRose had played on her. Frieta had all the money. Eddie had won a pot. Frieta had lied to her about that money. As yet she never had found out where Frieta had gotten it. Somehow, things were beginning to make sense to her now. Had Eddie seduced Frieta with the money? He was dirt enough for such a cursed act.

Alice turned towards the window. Sunshine greeted her harried face. For years she had tried to keep her daughter safe from all the hoodlums who had often kept company with her. One thing was certain. The baby did not belong to her music teacher. That was sure. It wasn't Charley's. Only one other person that she knew of had been with Frieta; a kid who had dated her at school. That had been nearly a year ago. For some reason she avoided men. Frieta hadn't seen the boy since he'd carried her to the College Fraternity dance. Anyway, Alice thought she was just crazy for thinking all that when she knew for certain that she half suspected it was Eddie LaRose who was responsible. A long shot would tell.

Turning from the window, she saw Frieta lift her head and their eyes met.

Alice's voice was frantic, full of threat and her own hurtful feelings.

"It's Eddie's isn't it?" she said. "It's his'n, isn't it, Frieta? It's his…. it's Eddie's! isn't it?… Tell me th' truth…. it's Eddie's!"

She had caught Frieta by surprise. Before the girl knew it she had blurted out,

"Oh, Alice…. Alice… he made me! He made me!"

Alice staggered over to the bed and dropped down before her. Teary-eyed, she gripped the girl's shoulders.

"You're lyin'. He never made you. You wanted him. You've always wanted all the dirty sonsofbitches I brought home. How did he make you? How, Frieta? How, I ask. How!"

"The money…. all that money!"

"How much did the dirty bastard entice you with? You certainly wouldn't have done it."

"A thousand dollars," Frieta bawled.

"I'll kill 'im. I'll kill that dirty sonofabitch if it's th' last thing I ever do!"

Frieta felt free to talk about herself now. The cat was out of the bag, and it was no longer a matter of secrecy. Frieta must acknowledge all.

"It's in me, Alice," she said. "I'm unable to stop myself. I'm sick. I'm a nymphomaniac!"

Alice looked at her hard and terrible.

"That time when I was drunk at that damned hotel, was Eddie with you all that time?"

Frieta nodded shamefaced, then dropped her head.

Alice could say no more. The terrible thoughts which possessed her tore into her soul. What a brute Eddie LaRose was. What a terrible beast she had taken up with. She had been warned, but she had merely disregarded McShane.

Mentally disturbed she turned away, covered her face and broke into sobs. Frieta watched her stagger out of the room. In the front room, Alice flung herself upon the divan and cried very distressfully. The room echoed with her hard sobs.

Frieta flung herself facedownwards upon the bed and sobbed along with her mother. Never before had she ever realized just how much Alice loved her.

CHAPTER TEN

B Y SIX IN THE EVENING the sun was blacked out by another heavy swirl of storm clouds which blew in from the west. Within a matter of an hour the threat of rain was again imminent.

Throughout the afternoon, Alice remained on the divan, much too depressed to move. Her mental capacity was blurred into haunting visions of the past month and how her daughter had been trapped by an unprincipled individual. She did not blame Frieta. It was all her own fault, and she was the one to stand the consequences. McShane had warned her against the man, but she had foolishly refuted him. Naturally it was very easy for the hoodlum to have Frieta if she was suffering from a sex-mania. Alice never imagined that her daughter could be a nymphomaniac. She had often come across various waitresses who related to her that they were that type who found it impossible to go for more than two days without a man. Once the man had kissed them the spark within them was quickly kindled and they found themselves unable to hold their bearings. Their morbid and ungovernable sexual craze must be appeased or they would find themselves in a tantrum of madness. Frieta must be saved.

At six-thirty Alice rose from the divan and went into the bathroom to wash and refresh herself. Then she returned to her bedroom and dressed and applied powder and saw to her makeup.

Noticing that the day had grown quite dark, she imagined that another rain storm was due. However, she did not imagine a rainstorm would disrupt her plans.

She opened the bottom dresser drawer and felt underneath a batch of linen until she found the .38 Caliber revolver. She thrust the gun into her purse. After getting a raincoat from the closet, she left the room.

Upon looking in on Frieta, she found her daughter asleep, so she closed the door softly and left the apartment.

Alice walked slowly down the stairs and left the apartment building. She turned east on Kansas Avenue, strolling along very jauntily. The wind was blowing, and already she felt the dampness in the air which meant that another rainstorm would come down within a matter of hours.

Her thoughts were not entirely her own. Certainly she never had any reason to commit murder before, despite what other individuals had done to her. She had never sought revenge before, not even when she had found herself pregnant many years ago in Waco, Texas. After all, the baby could be born and, somehow, survive the ugly conditions in which it had to live by being without a father. And she would never allow Frieta to have a child by Eddie LaRose. It would have been better for her to have his child than her own daughter. Even now, she could also be pregnant. Then that would make two of them which Eddie was guilty of. Mother and daughter.

Alice did not know why she wanted to murder Eddie LaRose. She could not deny the extreme hatred which she felt for him, and still she did not feel that she would be entirely satisfied by murdering the scoundrel. She felt a mean jealousy, for some reason. It cut into her soul, making her sick and bristling with animosity. She could not detest Frieta. She wasn't to blame. How many girls her own age would have refused a thousand dollars just for a few minutes of sensual love? Very few. And not any who felt their sexual desires ungovernable.

The main issue was that Eddie LaRose was nothing but a filthy rat, and in Alice's opinion no rat was fit to live in a decent society with individuals. She knew it would have been more appropriate to call in the police, but it was her own fight, and not theirs. Besides, the police would hardly do anything to Eddie for what he had done to Frieta. She had submitted to him, and she was no mere child. Frieta was quite grown.

Alice felt she had to kill him herself.

Within twenty minutes she had reached Third street and Kansas Avenue. The tavern was on the opposite side of the street. It was called Cowboy Inn. Eddie practically lived in the joint when he wasn't gambling. She knew he would be there. Yet her luck was even better. He was there at that particular moment.

As Alice paused to stare across the street at the joint, she observed Eddie's green Ford parked directly in front of the tavern. She could hear the music vendor playing. Some honky-tonk tune, it was.

She clutched her purse underneath her left arm and went across the street. A few drops of rain had commenced falling.

When Alice reached the car, she went over and looked inside. Just her curiosity, nothing else.

Nothing of interest was inside the car. A black pair of leather gloves were lying carelessly along the front seat, and a neatly wrapped package on the rear seat. The black gloves did not interest Alice, but the package did. To her it looked like nice gin, all labeled and bottled. Her kind, no doubt. Eddie always bought her kind. But her taste wasn't for gin right now. Not his. She wanted his blood, his life. She wanted to see him lying flat in the street, just like the rat he was. That was the only thing which would satisfy her at this particular moment.

Undaunted, she turned away from the car, taking slow steps towards the tavern door.

Alice pushed the paneless door and entered the tavern.

The joint wasn't very crowded. Most of the drinkers were seated in back booths. A couple were along the lower section of the bar, and two men were up front near the door, closer to her.

She did not see Eddie anywhere. Maybe they gambled down-stairs. If so, that's where Eddie was.

She went over and slipped on a stool. The barman's name was Luke, and he knew her. Why shouldn't he. She had been there many times with Eddie, drinking.

Luke was fat with a slouched belly and little pig eyes. He always carried a stubby cigar between the right side of his mouth. It was there now.

"Well, my friend, Alice," he grinned at her, drawing a wet towel across the counter before her.

Alice looked at his soiled jacket and stained apron. She forced a dry smile.

"How'dy, Luke," she said.

"What'cha gonna have, baby?" he asked. "But if yuh jest lookin' for Eddie, he's downstairs." He paused, leaned forward and whispered, "In a game."

She didn't reply to that. She just eyed the fat bartender and said,

"Gimme a rye and soda, Luke."

"Sure will, Baby," he said, and turned to fix the rye and soda.

Luke had Alice's drink before her in a jiffy, and she paid him. He rung up the money and started dumping some ice on the bottled beer. Alice contented herself to wait. She sipped the drink very carefully. Luke kept looking at her, obviously, noticing her darkened eyes, and that she appeared to have been involved in a row of some kind. But that wasn't anything unusual for the dames he usually met at the bar. Some of them were in much worse shapes after they had come off drunks and their old men had given them a working over with his fists.

Eddie came up quicker than Alice had calculated. Before she had half finished the drink, he was easing on the vacant stool on her left side, and laying an arm about her shoulders in a tenderly gesture.

"Well—well, Alice," he spoke nicely. "What a break, sugar. I was jest thinkin' 'bout you, baby."

She looked round at him, getting his strong masculine odor. Her heart fluttered, yet she was not discouraged by his presence. His hard eyes seemed more evil, and his features harmed by extreme dissipation. He didn't look clean one bit, and she imagined he had been hurt as much as she had by their savage brawl.

"I don't want anything to do with you, Eddie," she said. Somehow, she felt herself grown warm at the last minute, when she wanted to spit in his face, pull the weapon and blow his brains out.

"Alice, sugar," he said, more apologetic now. "God, I'm sure sorry 'bout what I did. Honest, babe. It's drivin' me nuts. Mah conscience's been botherin' me ever since. I cursed mahself night and day. Drunk for a week when I left the can. I hurt bad for what I done, Alice."

She frowned at him. "Save your grief for your old lady," she said coldly. "All I come in for was a drink. Then I'll get outa your sight."

She felt that her disinterest in him would suck him in. She wanted him away from the tavern, so she awaited her chance. He must never know that Frieta was pregnant. Never!

"Alice, please, babe," he groaned. "Look at me. I been sufferin', I tell you. I have. Honest."

"You're breakin' my heart," she snarled. "If you was so sorry why didn't you phone and apologize?"

"I wanted to. Really, babe. Honest."

She studied his unshaven face, his long hair and animalish expression. Indeed he looked more a bum than ever before.

"What're you after now? A skirt. You want your kicks, is that it? A free piece. Your lies don't stick with me, Eddie."

"Please, Alice. I admit it. I do. I'm no good. Rotten and dirty. I'm punished. Can't you forgive a person?"

"Sure. If you was a person. But you ain't. You're a rat. A dirty low-down rat. Now, beat it!"

He looked pitifully at her, and she felt her heart quiver for need of him. Did she actually want to murder Eddie? Now a different feeling had her heart. Murder was not really the thing she wanted. Despite what he had done to her daughter, and even to her, she loved him. He could actually have her again, despite all that had happened. Her heart melted at the very sight of him. She was a loving woman, not a brutal murderous one. What would she do if she had no one, when the feeling came on her again? Would Duke Wayne actually fall for her? Could she trust him? She didn't actually feel that she even wanted a cop for a lover. Some reason she didn't find them as free-hearted as other men. They had rules which had to be kept, and obligations, as well. Such would have to respect the law, and she didn't feel that she would be as free as she had been most of her life.

She looked at him, blushing, feeling composed as she had always been towards him.

"You know I was so kind to you, Eddie," she said regretfully. "Of all the guys I ever knew, well, I loved you th' most. You treated me real bad, real nasty. You didn't ever love me. You lied in order to satisfy yuh kicks."

"I'll beat it," he said, realizing that she had him all measured out. "I'll scram." He turned to leave, but she caught his arm.

"I'm not workin'," she told him. "I got fired. Maybe t'was my own fault, maybe not. I don't really know. If you was to help me along now and then, maybe I'd believe that you meant to do right this time. That is, if you care to patch things up and make a try at it again?"

He grinned slyly, unmindful of such clairvoyance of her.

"Alice, I love you, babe," he grinned, thinking she had turned soft towards him again.

The bartender came over and spoke to Eddie. Eddie nodded at him. The vendor stopped playing. Eddie put another quarter in the counter machine and the music started again.

"Don't hand me that bull," Alice sneered. "It makes my guts turn over when I hear you tellin' such a damn lie as that."

"You don't believe me, babe?"

"How can I believe you? Every time you open your mouth you're tellin' a goddamned lie."

He grinned at her. "Are you broke, now, babe?"

"Does it make any difference?"

"I've got fifty bucks."

"On you?"

"At my room?"

"Where's that?"

"Same place. Eighteenth and Kansas."

"Little good it'll do me at your room."

"We can go there, Alice."

"That a suggestion?"

"You need the money, don't you?"

"That's right. But I don't trust you."

"I promise you. Just ride over with me and I'll give it to you."

"There's no catch in it?"

"On my word, babe."

"Can I trust you, Eddie?"

"Do you want it or not?" He was adamant now.

Alice had been smoking. She looked up into his dark eyes and felt her heart throb for him as it always had. She mashed the cigarette out and caught his arm.

"All right, I'll go," she said.

They left the tavern, entered the Ford and he drove her directly to his room on Eighteenth and Kansas. She remained in the car while he hurried inside to get the money. In a few minutes he returned to the car, climbed behind the wheel and tossed five ten's on her lap. Alice took the money and smiled at him. She stuck it inside her bosom, not wishing to open her purse for fear he would spy the revolver. The money gave her a greater hope for their affair.

Eddie did not drive back towards the apartment as she had hoped he would. Instead, he turned westward and pressed on the gas, sending the Ford along at fifty miles an hour. Rain started dropping hard now.

"Where on earth are you takin' me, now?" she wanted to know. "I have to get back to Frieta."

"Frieta can wait," he said. "Just for a little spin. No harm, is there? Thought you'd like a little fresh air in the rain. You been in more than two weeks now."

Alice looked over at him, but she did not answer. His suggestion to take a ride was not the least unfavorable. She needed some fresh air, and a view of the country. This time of year it was beautiful. Things were growing. Farmers would not appreciate all the rain, however. It would ruin many of their crops, complete washouts.

Eddie was telling her how he obtained the liquor which he had in the back seat. Four fifths. Scotch. And he had won it gambling this morning. Some jerk had stolen the stuff from a drug-store and gambled it against five bucks at a crap game. He'd won the money and the fifty-dollars, besides.

After traveling five or more miles straight west on Highway-32, Eddie turned the car to the left off the highway and proceeded along a gravel road which wound and twisted through a corn field on the right side just off from the Kaw River, and there was a high bluff on the left side which boasted three wide layers, each higher than the other. The steep elevation twisted with the road, as it wound back southwards, curving slightly back east as they proceeded. There was not a house in sight. Only the com field, the river beyond on the southwest, and the high weedy bluff which extended ninety or a hundred feet vertical. Many shrubs were along the bluff, and heaps of weedy substances which at various sections were taller than the average man.

On both sides of the gravel road were deep gullies, and it took an expert driver to keep to the road. It was slippery due to the rain, and Eddie cursed for having not used his senses on such a nasty rainy evening. He had brought Frieta out here some while back, and he found it a very pleasant view to relax and watch the river. Here, the mind could dismiss all the vicissitudes of life and find consolation in nature's riot pleasures.

The rain was beating down now. Eddie had to stop the car before he reached the curve which to turn around. He parked and swore again.

Alice looked round, making a comment on how high the Kaw River was. Then she noticed the corn field. The corn stalks were nearly twelve to fifteen feet, and so dense and sodden that it seemed impossible to be penetrated.

"I thought we could talk better out here, Alice," he said to her, reaching over the seat to get the package of scotch.

Alice had forgotten her first intention to murder the man. In fact, she did not have any inclination to harm him at all now. She had relented to her impulse to try to forgive him. Taking a human life was not in her system. Some way she and Frieta could manage. She knew Eddie would never be of any use for her any more when it came to marriage. And Frieta certainly would never marry him, not after she had taken her to a good female specialist and had her administered for her mania for sexual desire.

"How 'bout a drink?" he asked, ripping off the cap of one bottle. He placed the remaining bottles of liquor back upon the rear seat.

Alice grinned, and took the liquor. She tilted the bottle to her lips, taking a gulping swallow. When she removed the bottle, she gave a luscious sigh and smiled softly over at him.

"Boy, that's real gone, honey," she commented pleasantly. She handed him the bottle, and he took his share and relaxed.

"Drink some more," he said politely, returning the bottle to her a second time. Alice took it and took another drink. He took another, until the bottle was empty. Then he lowered the window and hurled the empty bottle into the gully. It splashed in the water along the gully and sank.

Eddie leaned towards her, pulling her over into his arms. Deeply, he kissed her.

"Still mad at me?" he asked slyly.

"Not as much as I was at first."

"You feel good?"

"I'm okay."

He ran a hand along her left thigh. Then felt her breasts. He kissed her again. Alice felt herself trembling, and desire springing inside, a burning in her stomach made her sigh and she felt him, caressingly.

Now his hands moved along the bareness of her thigh. She didn't wear any stockings, nor panties, just a girdle. Her thighs were firmly held by the elastic material. The warmness of her body made her anxious to spread out for him so he could reach all of her.

"It's been three weeks, Alice," he whispered to her. "Three horrible weeks. Think of that!"

She looked at him, shivering as his hands found the edge of the girdle. He jerked it free from the side of her thighs, and she felt a cold breeze moving along her warmness. His palm was between her, forming a friction against her. She squirmed in the seat, rotating her hips nervously.

"Oh, Eddie. I want to.... I want to, but please...I don't know." She pushed him away, thinking what a wretched fool she was. "No, Eddie.... No, please." She looked down again at what he was showing to her. She felt miserable as the pressing lust overwhelmed her.

He reached for her again, contacting her arms and drawing her against his body. Before she could withdraw he had unfastened her blouse, and eased her brassiere from around her breasts. Her clothing shifted. Her body yearned for his contact. Her soul bled for sensual pleasure.

"No, Eddie," she said cruelly. "Don't be ridiculous!"

He shoved her over on the front seat, taking time to adjust himself, forcing her thighs apart. She struggled to get herself back upright. He contacted her. Then she struck him. She shoved him back. Her body went suddenly cold, repulsive, hard, uncivil, averse to him.

"Please, Alice," he rasped. "I need you. Oh, baby, don't be that way."

She adjusted her clothes, pulled her brassiere back over her breasts and started fastening her blouse back up. He was still feeling along her thighs, hoping she'd relent and satisfy him.

"Turn this rattle trap round and drive me back to town," she said bluntly. "I ain't no free pickings for you any more, Eddie. Don't feel on me. I can't do it. I just can't!"

Upon seeing her adamant disposition, he reached another bottle of liquor. He opened it and handed it to her. He had to get her drunk to make her act sensible.

"Take another drink," he said.

She shoved the bottle back. "Save it for yuhself," she said indifferently. "Take me back home."

"Don't be that way, Alice. God, I'm no bear."

"Please, Eddie, take me back to town."

She was overcome by the brutish manner which he had beaten her. Also, she was thinking about Frieta at the apartment. Pregnant. Carrying this dirty bastard's child. What a stupid idiot she was. What a sex-crazed bitch. She suddenly hated herself. Tears formed in her eyes. She felt nauseated as thoughts of her giving herself to him again pounced into her mind.

Eddie made no effort to start the car. In fact it was raining so hard that he couldn't have moved it one way or the other, anyway. He took several drinks, staring disgustedly over at her, hoping he wouldn't have to do what was in his mind to do in order for her to give herself to him.

Alice remained silent also. She imagined he was angry because she had repulsed him. She had found her nature entirely different than she had been before for him. The flame was gone, and could not be rekindled.

She looked over at him. He was drinking silently, hardly paying any attention to her.

"Listen," she said, "I'll walk back, if you don't mind. I'll climb out in the rain and find my own way back to the highway. Maybe somebody'll give me a lift into town. Sorry to have bothered you. Thanks for the money. I sure need it. Don't be angry at me, Eddie. I just can't do it any more. I'm silly, I guess. I had frightfully cold chills when you touched me a moment ago."

When he gave no answer, she opened the door and started out. He dropped the bottle, reached for her. He jerked her back into the car.

"Don't be a sap, Babe," he snarled. "I'll take you back as soon as I can turn the car round." It was merely a tricky statement, in order for him to get her back inside of the car.

Alice believed him. Perhaps he was on the level. He couldn't have reverted himself so suddenly. Actually, she felt that he could still be sorry and repentant for his past misdeeds. She had really forgiven him. Her first intention had been to murder the rat. However, her heart had conceived to mercy, and such a thought did not occupy her mind any longer. Certainly any other man, in his place, might have done the same thing to a girl in such a morbid sexual state as Frieta had been.

As Alice turned back to the seat and closed the door, he reached for her. His seizure was contrary to gentleness which had been in his voice. Brutally, he jerked her back into his arms. Her head crashed against his chest. For a moment, she saw stars, yet she struggled to free herself. She turned startled eyes on him.

"Eddie, for heavens sake!" she cried. "What's th' matter with you?"

"I never drove out here to be put off," he snarled. Before she could answer, he had ripped her blouse open, trying to peel her rain coat from her shoulders. She beat at his mad hands, repulsing him as much as she could.

He pulled her off the seat. She sprawled backwards on the floor, her skirt pulled back along her thighs. The girdle had already been torn free of her legs, therefore he had complete access to her if he once got her in a sprawling position.

The enclosure in the front seat was much too small in order for him to take her properly. But he shoved her head towards the floor, and pulled her legs up towards the seat. Otherwise, Alice suddenly found herself nearly on her head. Her rain coat and skirt dangled over her face and arms. Her thighs were free. She could feel the cold air licking at her exposed flesh.

"Eddie, stop it!" she demanded. "Please, don't hurt me!" She tried to kick his arms, but he held both her legs to both sides of his body. She had a glimpse of him with his trousers peeled down. He was making the contact. But his nose was bleeding. His tongue was licking the dripping blood which flowed freely from his nose. She had not realized that she had scratched and bruised his nose until she had spied the blood. She realized he might be angry enough to kill her now.

Even while he contacted her, pressing himself until she could feel sensual pangs, sweetness surging into her soul. Yet the evilness of his past and present, surged forth into her brain. He was actually raping her, taking her against her will. What a dirty bastard he was, she thought. The previous fracas she had had with him pounced into her memory, making her soul cold and effortless to his present undulations against her body.

Fear, intermingled with hatred, made her dizzy and rebellious. She didn't think he intended to let her back to town alive. That was why he was attacking her.

Had Eddie actually lured her out here with the money in order to murder her this time?

CHAPTER ELEVEN

A LICE FOUND HERSELF TREMBLING and giving herself to him. The contact was not altogether reality for her, but vague and hollow, more like a forceful aggression of love. If she could have gotten her purse from underneath her shoulders she would have taken out the gun and shot him to death in the very emotional contact which he was in.

As the feeling grew into her soul, she kicked her legs and pressed herself back against the door. He was whining, making quick grunts as the thrill poured into his warm veins. She was working her thighs anxiously, pressing herself towards him, seeking the sweetness. She wanted it now. Yet she hated it. However she could not defeat the sweetness. Her lips were drawn back. Her eyes were closed. She could vision all kinds of luscious feelings in her confused mind.

Alice was pressing herself away from him. She had determined to dissuade his complete fulfillment. No release on her part. She would kill that effort if nothing else. She'd cheat the sonofabitch when he reached the stage of utter and savage release.

As she pressed away, he fell down upon her. He was breathing heavily, more like a sex maniac. He put fear into her soul, more than the sensation of love which he might have thought he was doing.

Suddenly the door on her side flew open. She had already felt the five ten's seeping out loosely from her bosom where she had placed it earlier. Evidently the door had not been locked sufficiently when she closed it.

As the door opened, rain and wind licked at her face and she felt the coldness of her nakedness. Looking up at Eddie, she could see his lusty face, absorbing her as he always had, only he was taking her against her will this time. Other instances she had given her body to him.

The money was suddenly sucked up by the wind and rain, and she noticed it fluttering over her head and out the car. Rain caught hold of the greenbacks and hurled them into the watery gully beside the gravel road.

With the door open she had a chance to pull herself away from his contact. He was holding her, taking her fully. His undulations were more energetic. He was racing towards the complete satisfaction. She could hear him snorting.

Alice disregarded him altogether now. Hers was not near exploding. The feeling was sweet, but it was, also, bitter. She reached over her head, her fingers seized the car chassis. Her face was flushed, greatly dismayed and frustrated. She saw the animal expression he wore. It was about to happen. His eyes were closed, envisioning the tense pleasure.

As she saw his lips part to taste the final outcome, she gave a savage jerk with her arms and body. His contact was instantly broken. And he looked to see her tumbling out the car upon her head and shoulders.

Her naked thighs were still exposed as she landed head-on against the rain-soaked earth. However, she scrambled to her feet, pulling her skirt and coat over her body, adjusting her blouse. Brushing straggling hair from her face. In doing so, she nearly slipped over into the gully beside the road. Only a sudden leap prevented her from falling into the gully.

Gasping and brushing rain from her face, Alice staggered impotently to the car's rear fender and paused, looking through the right side window at her puzzled and disappointed attacker. She still clutched her purse. She thanked God for that.

"You dirty sonofabitch!" she screeched. "You're no good. Eddie, I hate you ... oh, I hate you .... You dirty dog ... you raping hoodlum!"

It was difficult to reason whether it was her taunting curses, or the fact that he had been so dully cheated from his kicks, which spurred his mad actions. Actually, he had been so pleasantly devoted to his sensual release, until he was nearly stunned when she had sprang away from him. He had never thought a woman capable of breaking such a sexual contact when his was about to happen.

The rain was nearly blinding. Thunder growled. Alice was getting soaking wet.

Eddie LaRose jerked his head round first, then twisted his entire body, leaning forward in the seat until he saw where she was standing. Then a savage impulse sent him bounding out the car.

As the man leaped out the door and his feet struck the soggy ground, his left foot took a nasty slip. He lost his balance and went sliding on his rump, over into the deep gully which Alice had managed to avert.

That pleased Alice. She laughed, taunted him more with curses. In all the abusement she had actually forgotten about the gun inside her purse. She did not feel that she wanted to kill, anyway. No matter how cruelly she was dealt, it seemed that she got somewhat of a thrill from it. The pains she suffered from her lovers meant something to her. After all, he gave her fifty dollars. Was that why he felt that he was cheated so badly, and actually took her against her will. Maybe she was to blame for his uncouth actions.

Eddie's curseful oaths explained just how mean and vicious he felt. He made an effort to climb out of the gully, but each time he slipped back. His fingers could get no firm grip against the muddy side of the bank.

Alice did not wait to see how he was going to get himself clear of the gully. She tucked her rain coat snugly about her body, pulled the hood over her head and started walking fast along the water-puddled gravel road back northwards, towards Highway-32.

Thunder roared. The earth trembled. Streaky flashes of lightning illuminated the sky. Rain poured down in a raging torrent. The old road was a stream of watery-gravel and sticky grey clay. Alice's high-heels sank over her ankles, and her feet were soggy wet. It was a burden as well as a hindrance to her. She realized that it was over two miles back to the highway. She wondered if she could make it all in one part.

Her thoughts were a jumble of discomforts. Things which, she assumed, were part of the cruel moments of life. In no imaginative dream would she have seen herself having another affair with Eddie LaRose. Still it had happened. She felt unclean and foul. How rotten could she get. After what he had done to Frieta, her own daughter. Murdering him was not the solution. If Frieta had the baby, at least if he was alive he could help support it. Yet the thoughts of Frieta having his baby was the bitter pill which nauseated her. How could she prevent it without destroying a life? Could Frieta lose it, someway? Something had to happen. The bold sense of all was so unpleasant to think.

She was hurrying along as fast as she could walk. Oftentimes, she stumbled, her feet slipping about the watery road, but she managed to maintain her pace.

Suddenly she heard someone directly behind her. The hard rain and constant thunder had been so violent until she had failed to notice anyone behind her. Not that close.

Wheeling, she confronted Eddie LaRose!

He was just about fifteen feet away from her. How senseless was she to allow the brute to sneak up on her until he was that close on her. She had turned a slight curve, and during that interval she had not had a chance to see him.

So startled was she, until she lost her step while making a quick motion to flee away from him. Her high-heels tripped her and she tumbled over into the middle of the filthy roadbed.

As he approached her with a naked grin, she noticed the long shiny-bladed knife which he held in his waist. It was jammed through his belt loop, so that it showed plainly. He was soaking wet, his trousers all besplattered and soiled with slimy grayish-brown mud and clay. His shoes were caked with clumps of mud. He looked a hideous madman.

"Get up," he snarled, catching hold of one of her arms. "We're goin' back to the car."

Slowly she staggered to her feet, clutching her purse. She looked into his coldblooded eyes. There was no consolation in his cold defenseless stare. At that particular moment she hated herself for ever thinking of finding him again. How could she have ever imagined that this man had a forgiving and kind heart such as hers. Being so loving, she trusted everyone. Forgave them, as well. Not this brute. He was one who could never be forgiven. One must hate and detest him forever, eternal. There was no good in him. McShane's diagnosis of his case had been solidly true. He was a criminal who could never reform. He had a bewitched mind of contaminated evil. It was the mind of the ruthless infidel.

"Let me go, Eddie!" she demanded. "I don't wish to go back to your car. Let me go home, please!"

"We goin' back and finish what I started," he threatened. "Come on!" He shoved her along, back towards the car. She went a little ways and stopped again, crying now, afraid of him. He had never showed himself so outright brutish before, only when he had jumped on her. And she had been to blame for that. She had struck him first when he had merely been trying to kiss her.

"Eddie, please," she begged. "I don't want to go back. I don't want to do it. You've already hurt me. My legs are crampin' th' hell outa me. I'm wet and cold. Look at my feet. How do you think I feel? Don't you have any kind of mercy for me, or even yourself. Let's go back home. We can dry ourselves out there. Maybe then, it'll be better."

His expression showed no remorse. Before she could speak again, he slapped her, knocking her to one knee. She dropped her head and sobbed. He caught one arm and yanked her up to her feet.

Without a word he gripped her arm and started shoving and pulling her brutally on back down the road, back towards the parked Ford.

He wasn't talking as he jerked and yanked her along. He was walking very fast, as if something, in particular, was tempting his mind. She was half running, stumbling in order to keep up with him.

"Eddie, please…please!" she begged. "I'm really sick. I'm 'bout to die, I feel so bad."

He looked cruelly at her. "Didn't I tell yuh to drop it!" With a gesture he slammed his fist against the side of her head. She staggered again, and fell. Roughly, he yanked her back to her feet.

She was crying hard and could hardly see or think of what she was doing, and certainly not where she was going. If she ever got out of this alive, she swore she would never again take up with drinking hoodlums. Eddie was drunk for one thing, and he was murderously angry for another. She had to get away from him. She felt that his intentions were to strip her all the way down this time, and take her right. Make her pay dearly for the devilish manner which she had cheated him before. She wondered what he would do to her after he had finished with her. Would he actually cut her throat? He had the knife. It frightened her, and made her want to obey him until she had her chance to squirm out of the mess.

When they arrived back at the car, he opened the back door and shoved her inside. She sprawled on her face upon the seat, and he climbed in behind her and shut and locked the door.

He watched her a moment, very carefully, while she pulled herself erect and started wiping her wet face on her skirt. She kicked off her wet shoes, and adjusted her rain cape from over her head.

He had a bottle of liquor again, raising it to his lips, taking a big drink. When he had satisfied himself, he offered her the bottle.

"No ... no, I don't want a drink," she whined. She continued to cry, silent tears which showed how hurt and dejected she was for having ever trusted Eddie LaRose a second time.

"I said drink!" he threatened.

In order not to get another mauling against her head, she took the bottle of liquor from him and slowly raised it to her lips. She did not drink enough, so he reached over and gave her a nice shove to remind her that he wasn't kidding.

She drank her fill and returned the bottle to him. Then he drained the bottle and lowered the window and hurled it out into the gully.

"Eddie, can I talk to you?" she whined. "Let me say somethin' to you, please?"

He raised his hefy head and leered at her. "Say it, then," he told her. "And after you say it start shuckin' down. We gonna finish what we started. I mean it, Alice."

"Are you really mad at me?"

"I could kill you!"

"Why, Eddie? What have I done to you?"

"You givin' me a brush-off. I don't go for no goddamned brush-off from no lousy broad, see!"

"No I'm not. Eddie, I love you. I want you, but not here. Not like this!"

"Strip down. All th' way. I'm gonna take you all night I'll teach you to run out on me, givin' me a damn brush-off." He started removing his jersey and kicked off his muddy shoes.

Rain was beating down on the top of the used Ford, making a deafening racket. It was dusky dark, now. Nightfall was very near. To the right the corn stalks waved and bowed their tassels under the heavy pounding of rain. A dense mist lay in that direction, obviously coming from the river. Far away, towards the west, came the mournful whistle of a streamliner. The hills to their left were gushing torrents of muddy water, which whirled down deep crevices along the hillside.

Alice gave a hard blow, watched Eddie's hairy chest as he slung his jersey aside.

Slowly, she started undressing in the back seat. Nauseated pangs drew her body together. She choked, swallowing hard, biting her lips. Tears ran from her eyes in her prolonged nervousness.

Slowly her thoughts turned towards religion. Something the minister had said at Mike Hernden's funeral. 'While living the soul bears the strains of a meager purgatory, but in death such a purgatory reverts into a bounding and heavenly glory.'

Alice looked over at Eddie again. That part of him which she had so humbly cherished in past days did not seem like flesh at all to her. While the liquor had stimulated his passions instantly, it had only created a deep feeling of frightful animosity for him in her.

"Eddie, please, don't make me," she whined. "At home, yes. Even a hotel room. Not here. Not this barbaric insensible way!"

In response to her, he reached over and tore her blouse down and yanked her skirt along her legs until he had it clear of her body. She could smell his foul breath, the vulgar sneering of his parted lips.

"Shuck down, I say," he growled.

An involuntary motion of his part to get another bottle of liquor off the floor gave her the chance she had been half expecting. He was crouched over towards her, feeling beneath her legs for the other two bottles of liquor. The moment he took his eyes off her, her left hand reached quickly, frantically desperate, for the doorknob. In a swift gesture, she swung the door open and flung herself out upon the ground, bringing her dangling skirt and her purse along with her.

In the rainy mud she staggered to her feet. Her skirt sagged along her lower limbs, so she kicked it free, and fled only in bra and girdle and her bare feet. In her fanatic haste, she still clung to the purse. It was her weapon of defense. Her only means to save herself if Eddie should not control himself.

Alice ran towards the right side of the road, her objective was the corn field. Once over there she could hide from him. Maybe she would die of pneumonia after the effects of the soaking which she would surely get, but it might save her the trouble of having to murder Eddie.

She leaped the gully, fell to her knees in the mud, dropped her purse, then picked it up and staggered on, her feet sinking half the length of her limbs as she trudged into the thick slimy mud and water.

Behind, she heard him splashing through the mud after her. This time he was bedeviled with rage and furious murder.

Within a matter of seconds, Alice was dripping wet, her cold body shivering like a freezing dog. Her hair soggy wet, dangling to her shoulders. Her teeth chattered, and her nerves were near collapsing.

Before she was twelve feet from the corn stalks, she turned to see where he was. He was just skirting the gully beside of the road. But he was coming with great leaps and bounds. He was desperate, fierce and murderously inclined!

She wheeled to run into the corn stalks. The moment she turned, she stepped accidently off into a deep gully, overflowing with rain water. It had been to dark for her to notice.

As she fell down, she gave a curt, wild scream, and felt herself sinking to her knees. Slipping and trying to steady herself, she climbed out on the other side of the slimy pit, and fell weakly upon the ground in the mud and water. There she lay like a crippled female animal, unable to budge, too tired, too frightened. She waited for him to deal out the punishment to her which she knew he would give her for her rebelliance and repulsiveness.

She held her purse in both hands, savoringly. She sobbed hysterically. Vaguely she saw him skirt around the bog hole which had tripped her. She knew her left ankle was slightly sprung. That was the reason she couldn't get to her feet to avoid him.

He paused ten feet from her with his naked body off balanced, and undoubtedly cold and uncomfortable from the rain. In his right hand, he gripped the handle of the long blade.

At that moment, lightening flashed. Thunder rumbled. The ground trembled. Alice bowed her head and prayed. She sensed that she must either kill or be killed. She had no other alternative. Reasoning with Eddie LaRose was entirely out of the question. He appeared hopelessly insane. It was much too dark now for her to see his face, but she could still see his dim form lingering there, as though he was waiting for her to rise, so he could plunge the sharp steel into her heart!

"Eddie, honey," she pleaded. "Eddie, do you hear me, honey. Oh, please, don't do this to me!"

He didn't reply. His stalk silence added more horror to the ghastly scene.

"I'll go back to the car with you, honey," she pleaded. "I'll do anything you want me to. Honest. I won't run away no more. You can have me, honey. You can have me. Don't you understand what I'm sayin' t'you?"

He made no movement, neither did he make any sound. Then he started moving slowly towards her, and she could sense the murderous intention which he possessed.

"Take me, Eddie. Right here. It don't matter. Don't dare kill me. Eddie, I'll do it. I will. I will, honey!"

"You dirty whore!" he snarled contemptuously. "I'm gonna rip it outa you. Givin' me th' slip. Goddamn you!"

She cowered back. The rain nearly made her blind. Yet she cowered back, pulling herself along the mud and wet weeds. She kept her purse in her hands. Possessed with strangling fear, she dare not make a motion to open it. One movement and he would lunge down upon her, and start jabbing away with that sharp blade.

"Eddie, you really gonna kill me, aren't you?" she bellowed. "Takin' Frieta. You took her. Didn't you know she told me that? She's knocked up. You give her a baby. She's got it. How do you think I feel by you doin' all that t'me? That's why I'm actin' so crazy, honey. I keep thinkin' how you tricked me in order to go to my little girl and enjoy her just because she's sick and can't help herself. Eddie, God, have mercy on me. I don't wanna die. I don't. I don't! Let's stop it. You can have me, I told you that. I'll be real gentle with it!"

"Beg you bitch!" he growled. "Beg for your stinkin' life. See if it helps."

"Listen, I'm freezing like this. All this water fallin' on us. Can't we go back to the car. We can talk inside the car, Eddie."

He had paused again. She was so nervously upset until she didn't know whether she had stalled his deadly intentions or not.

Before she knew it, she found herself on her feet. That was why he had been waiting. For her to rise up to her feet. He couldn't kill a female while she was on the ground. He was low, but not that low.

The moment Alice stood, he lunged at her. The blade struck her right shoulder. She felt the thrusting throbs of pain, then she saw him slip as he made another effort to bring the blade towards her throat. He fell over to the left, while she sank on one knee. Her shoulder bled profusely.

"Takin' my little girl, knockin' her up wasn't 'nough, was it?" she groaned. "Beatin' me nearly t'death for practically nothin' after that. Why that, Eddie? Bringin' me out here to this deserted corn field, tryin' to rape me. All that dirt, and it makes you better than me. You're drunk, but you're not too drunk to kill me. You want my blood for my love, not for what I've done to you. You can have me all you want, but God knows you'll never touch Frieta again. I'm gonna die tryin' to save her from a dirty dog as you, Eddie."

He had found his legs underneath his body again. Upright, he made his murderous way towards her a second time. Only his form could she see, but he was certainly there. Ready to finish her off.

Alice finally gathered her courage and fumbled frantically with her purse. Eddie kicked her over, then stood back. She was dazed, somewhat, yet she was revived by the cold rain, and did not pass out entirely.

She did not know when the gun had come into her hands. Anyway it was there, suddenly. He was coming at her again, unaware that she was even armed.

She had leaning over on her elbows with the gun pointed up at him. Obviously, he made out the weapon. He made a quick motion to reach her with the knife. Then she fired!

As the bullet struck him, Eddie paused. Then she fired again. He staggered. Gunsmoke drifted around them, forcing it's way though the heavy rain. Then Alice dropped the gun. She watched Eddie staggering away from her. Something thudded against the mud at his feet. The knife. Rain beat down heavier, ridiculously. Alice covered her face and screamed hysterically.

CHAPTER TWELVE

FATALLY WOUNDED, Eddie LaRose staggered away from Alice until he had reached the stalks of corn.

Alice quivered against the hideous rain and sloppy earth. Now she removed her hands from her face and looked across at Eddie. She saw him stagger into the tall com. His heavy body crushed and snapped the stalks. Then he fell with a heavy thud. One dying groan was uttered from his foul lips. Then nothing else. Only the beating rain and the rustle of the weather against the earth and corn stalks.

Eddie's silence hurt Alice. She cried harder. Once when lightning flashed, she spied the path of his fatal walk. She felt impotently weak. Her shoulder bled. The wound was disturbing her.

She had to get out of the cold and raw weather. However, she must go to Eddie first. She must help him. Maybe he was still alive. Maybe the bullets had only wounded him. She had to save him. She hadn't really wanted to kill him.

Weakly, Alice dug her fingers into the mud, then slapped the wet mud against her open wound. Somewhere she had read or heard that mud would hold the bleeding part of the body. Once she had fixed the mud over the shoulder wound, she pressed her left hand over the mud to hold it there. Then she staggered to her feet and plodded her way over towards the place where she had last seen her vile lover.

"Eddie!" she screeched. "Eddie!"

There came no reply, only the thudding rain and the rustle of the heavy corn stalks.

Her suspense nearly murdered her. Now she ran, more wild and disheveled than ever. Her near naked body was flushed and filthy with muddy particles. To her bone marrow, she felt the chilly discomfort. Her teeth chattered, and her skin tissues felt numb, and as if she was dreaming all this.

When she came upon Eddie's body, she stopped, clutched to a corn stalk to steady herself. He was lying flat on his face, his head completely submerged under a watery-puddle. Even if the shots had not been fatal to him, now his life was snuffed out. He was quite dead.

Alice fought her way to him, flinging herself down upon that part of his body which was visible.

"Eddie, honey," she said in a chilly tone, "speak to me. Eddie, please. I never intended to hurt you. You made me … oh, I didn't mean it … I didn't. I didn't!"

While Alice would hardly have shown any remorse for her crime had she been completely sober, under the circumstances, but she was half drunk. She was nearly wrecked, mentally. Reality was, somewhat, vague and imaginary to her.

At last she forced herself to her feet and staggered about in aimless circles until she finally found herself back at the car. She actually fell into the gully along the gravel road before she managed to get across it. Her fingers and arms looked raw white, only in the darkness, now, it was hardly visible. The young woman possessed a strong constitution, and the liquor she had consumed helped to keep her blood circulating enough to render her salvation enough to reach the car.

Once she had managed to get inside the car, she was able to rest and some senses returned to her.

Instinct, more than certainty, made her get behind the wheel. The motor had never been shut off. Eddie had left the motor running in order to keep the heater warm and the car comfortable for them. It was very warm and cozy inside the vehicle.

Alice made no attempt to remove her drenched underthings, her mind was set on getting back to the apartment. So she tried to turn the car around on the narrow rain-drenched road. Naturally it couldn't have been done. Not even by an expert and sober driver. Yet she tried. Only she hardly moved the car backwards before she had backed straight into the ditch. The car bounced. She was jostled over to the right side. There she fell backwards in the seat, started racing the motor, hearing the spinning wheels.

Realizing that the car was stuck in the gully, Alice discarded the idea of driving back to town. She reached over the back seat and found the remaining bottle of liquor. After managing to get the cap off, she drank crazily, hoping it would stimulate her enough to keep herself together until morning. Or would there be any morning for her? How would anybody know where she was, or where to look for her. The main issue which she was somewhat conscious of, was the fact that she had killed Eddie. A murder crime hung heavy over her head. The liquor would help her to eliminate thoughts of her cruel deed. It would completely take her into another world. Give her a boost into a dream world, if she drank enough of it. So she kept tilting the bottle to her lips. The car motor hummed. The rain beat constantly upon the top of the car. It was very warm in the front seat. The heater sent warmth against Alice's naked thighs, drying them out. Even her undergarments began to dry on her body.

The minutes passed. Then an hour. At last Alice dropped the whisky bottle to the floor and slumped over along the front seat with her head in the driver's seat. She had definitely passed out.

The rain beat down. Thunder growled. The car motor missed, once or twice. It's gas tank was empty and it stopped altogether. Yet, by now, Alice was hardly aware that she even existed. She lay motionless and as dead against the seat.

Alice had not been gone from the apartment more than an hour before Frieta awakened. She heard it raining and thought no more or less that another rain storm was in progress. Upon hearing no sound, and sensing that Alice must be asleep in another room, she climbed from bed and dressed into a cotton dress. Her stomach pains had ceased. She felt as good as ever, now.

At the dresser, Frieta turned on a lamp, saw to her make-up and combed her hair. She was thinking about her pregnancy. And she had a savoringly idea just what she was going to do about it. She would definitely get married. With the right man, she felt that all her morbid sickness could, at least, be solved. Her husband could satisfy her until she could be cured, that is, if there was a cure for her.

She was definitely going to have her baby. She wanted it, despite the fact that it might not be just right. If she put it up for adoption, it would be better than destroying it's life.

She entered the front room and turned on a light. She looked down at the divan where she had heard Alice sobbing, earlier. Two pillows were at one end of the divan, a dent was pressed on them, but her mother was not there. Neither was Alice in her bedroom, nor the kitchen. She had gone out, or was probably next door at Gladys's quarters.

Frieta crossed the room, opened the door and crossed over to Gladys's door. She knocked. There was no reply to her knocks, so she decided that Gladys wasn't home either. Maybe the two women left together. Anyway, it was nothing for her to get upset about. She had to look to her own wants, right now. A pressing urge was creating a morbid sickness in her which she could not appease on her own. No longer was she going to deny herself by self-indulgence. She must act according to her desires and fancies. She was already with child, so it didn't matter any longer just how much she did it to quench the savage thirst inside her body.

She returned to the bedroom and selected a transparent slicker from the closet. Bundling herself up very snugly, she called a taxi. Inside of twenty minutes the taxi-cab arrived and, taking her purse and umbrella, Frieta left the apartment.

She directed the cabman to drive her to Eighth and Barnet to Charley Boyles's apartment, and when the taxi reached the big apartment building, a few moments later, she paid her fare and alighted to run inside the vestibule out of the rain.

The self-service, just inside the hallway, was up on the sixth floor, so Frieta used the stairway at the left of the elevator shaft. Charley's rooms were on the third floor. It was no job for her to walk up.

Once at the apartment door, she pushed his doorbell and heard someone playing the piano. She recognized Charley's own style and nimble-fingered piano playing. She smiled, thinking how long she had postponed accepting his proposal. Now she would tell him the truth, and if he still wanted to marry her, she would accept him as her husband. She assumed Charley was a very potent man, despite being over forty. More than she could recall, he had teased her with caresses, and gentle pawings along her naked arms. How she had wanted to clutch him and demand that he take her, but she had felt too ashamed at the instances. No longer was she to halt the fierce love which he had for her. His great desires would be satisfied now, as well as her own fierce sensual thirst. Her body screamed for attention as she contemplated her daily fulfillment.

Charley opened the door, greatly surprised to see her standing there.

"Frieta, my dear," he said, taking her into his arms and closing the door. The apartment smelled sweet, of burning mild incense. Charley wore summer tights, and his chest was bare. Frieta knew he slept as he felt. He had a mania for nudity. Such a man was after her soul. She could not imagine why she had denied herself all such persistent demands of her body for so long. She hated herself for this foolish self-perservation.

"What's brought you out here so late, my dear?" he asked, guiding her towards the lavish front parlor. "I was just hoping someone would drop in to spend the evening. Rest your wraps, my lovely one."

She wished he wouldn't be so damn polite and timid towards her. Maybe that was the reason she had usually prolonged her sensual love since his wife had died.

Taking a seat on the settee, Frieta watched him take her things into the bedroom, then she sat down, picked a cigarette from the coffee table and lit it. She crossed her legs and was smoking when he returned to the room.

He sat down beside her and his light brown eyes seemed to sparkle with his queer delight in the dim lampglow.

"You're lonesome, aren't you, Charley?"

He dropped his head, but did not have any reason to reply. Instead, he said, "Care for a drink? I can fix you a high-ball, or martini?"

"No thanks," she smiled, watching his nervous and uneasy eyes. "My stomach has been upset all morning, honey. I'm afraid that drinks might make me ill again."

"That's too bad, Frieta. What's th' trouble?"

"For th' time being, lets just say an upset stomach."

"Want me to play for you? I was composing a new song when you rang the doorbell. Maybe you'd like to hear what I've written thus far?"

"I'll hear it another day," she said.

He frowned, unable to imagine just what was bothering her.

"Something wrong?" he asked.

"Something's always wrong with me," she said invitingly. She knew he'd never catch the hint.

"Well, that's natural in girls your age, dear one. You look very pretty, with your hair-do. I never realized you were so beautiful, Frieta."

Now he's getting warm, she thought. His wife certainly spoiled his lust for women. She must have been extremely cold-natured, Frieta imagined.

"What do you do all alone here at nights?" she asked. "Just play the piano and read all your books?"

"What can any man do who has no woman in his life. It's hellishly sickening, Frieta."

"Don't remind me," she said, watching the hard cue in his eyes. "I know what you mean, honey."

"Do you really?" he smiled, as if he thought she was lying.

"You bet, my dear."

"Of course you're not a man, Frieta. Women can find plenty lovers, but a man my age must be particular. My youth is gone. You're young and beautiful. Plenty young men would fall for you. How do you manage to avoid the young wolves?"

"That's easy. I stay shut in. How else? If they don't know I exist, there's nothing for me to worry about. But, getting back to the point. Honey, you're not old. Music and novels and with all your composing ability. Why, Charley, you're simply beautiful. You're something special to me." As she spoke she reached over and caressed his bare flank. His eyes went down to her long-tapering fingers, which felt so soft and tantalizing to him.

There was no need for her to pretend any longer. She felt the demanding thrust inside her, and her nerves leaped with a sudden jolting that made her ashamed. She looked into his eyes and caught her breath.

"Frieta, I love you," he said. He had finally sensed the feelings which possessed her. "Can the disparity of our ages harm us?"

"Charley, don't tease me," she nearly begged, "Nothing can harm us tonight!"

Slowly he leaned over towards her. Their eyes met, savoringly. He did not fail to notice the lusty temptations in her dark eyes. A magnet of sensualty was drawing them towards each other. Then, suddenly, she was in his arms. She felt him anxiously, and he caught her chin, turned her lips up and pressed his firmly upon hers. His mad desire for her had intensified. She had thought him capable, but never for once had she realized he was so virile, so strongly aggressive.

"I've wanted you terribly, Frieta," he moaned, as his tongue moved hotly along the slope of her throat, then paused at the edge of her bosom.

Frieta twisted herself backwards on the settee, brushing strands of hair from her face. Her exotic fragrance seemed to stimulate his violent passions to a seething peak. She felt her throbbing pulse.

"I've wanted you, too!" she began, pulling him down upon her. "Take me, Charley. Take me, please. Hurry… God, hurry!" Her words were uttered so impulsively and involuntarily, that he seemed paralyzed by her savage animal-like tone.

"Frieta! You're beautiful," he cried. "God!"

There was a daybed at the rear of the oblong room. Charley usually lounged there in the late afternoons when he had finished with his daily music teaching.

He picked her up and carried her over to the daybed. There, she quickly fumbled with her skirt and underthings until she was naked. Then she fell back upon the daybed, watching his bronze body looming over her. His naked flesh inflamed her passions.

She felt the eagerness beating inside her, and her voice was more demanding than ever.

"Hurry, Charley. Hurt me. Do it to me!"

He caught her and moved her gradually forward so that she was directly exposed to him. Her back arched. Her head was flung back in a manner which intensified the strain in her body. Her breasts shuddered as she felt the heated friction of his lips and tongue. She felt her burning buttocks, unable to stop the mounting pleasure. As fire leaped more wildly into her, she pushed herself forward, seized his head and flung herself energetically. She pressed herself, quickly undulating her hips madly up at him, making him take her with more renewed energy.

"Oh, please … please … so good … so good!"

He moved forward then. As he made the contact, her body became a rocket of quiverings and wildish convulsions which mounted by degrees as he insinuated himself quickly between her.

Suddenly she was crying and whining and laughing at the same time. She pressed her lips to him as the spasm of release sent her flanks towards the ceiling and made her kick and claw his arms and shoulders. His tongue parted her lips as she gave out, and she lay underneath him purring and moaning as the sensational feelings subsided.

Later they were kissing on the settee again. She had a desperate desire to spend the night with him, only she was afraid Alice might become worried about her. And she did not wish to cause her mother any more disturbances.

After they had showered and dressed, they entered the kitchen. Charley was a devoted bachelor when it came to fixing appetizing delicacies. He made Frieta sit at the table while he prepared a big dish of relish salad, and fried a catfish which he had been thawing since noon. It was just about eight o'clock, and Frieta had already phoned the apartment, but Alice hadn't answered. Therefore, she didn't see any need to hurry back home, since Alice wasn't there.

When the catfish was done, Charley sat the table and they had wine as an appetizer.

"Frieta," he said, "Will you marry me?" he proposed. "I love you, sweet one. I want you. I need you. Please, understand, baby."

She looked at him and smiled dreamily. "Do you really need me?" she asked with a trifle of pleasure in teasing him.

"You know I do."

"You know something, Charley."

"What, my love?"

"You may hate me after I tell you the truth."

"Nothing can make me hate you, baby. Nothing!"

She studied his smiling eyes. He was eating fish and sipping from his glass of wine.

"Did you notice how crazy I am?" she asked. The time was ripe to tell him the truth about her. She didn't know whether he would be disappointed in her after he found out or not. She had to have somebody. She must get married or maybe find herself with another man such as Eddie LaRose.

"I didn't think you were crazy," he denied. "You're a very sexual girl. I must admit."

"Charley, I'm sick."

"You told me that when you first came."

"No, no. I mean I'm sexually ill. I'm a nymphomaniac!"

He dropped his fish on the plate, eyed her with puzzled eyes. He was obviously unsure whether she was serious or not.

"Are you kidding?" he asked.

"Did I act like it?" she asked, and watched his thoughtful expression.

"No," he finally replied. Then he smiled. "So what? Any woman can find herself sick that way. Sometimes it's caused by various irritated conditions in the body. I might want you to even be that way, darling. I'm a very potent man. I have never found a woman who could satisfy me nearly enough."

"You mean you're that way, too?"

"I'm a white-livered man, Frieta. I never get enough."

She looked into his serious eyes, took a sip of wine and said, "I'll marry you, Charley. Anytime, you say so."

He smiled his acceptance, and lifted his wine glass in a toast to their future.

"But maybe I'd better tell you this first," she went on, watching his eyes turn more questioningly on her. She bit her lips, then dropped her head. Maybe she had better not tell him until he had finished eating. He might lose his appetite at the table as his appetite for her.

"What is it, sweet one?" he inquired. He could see the shame and hurt lingering in her baby-blue eyes. He rose from the table and hurried to her. Frieta had begun to sob. Teardrops oozed along her fair cheeks.

Beside her he lifted her up into his arms. "What on earth's wrong?" he inquired uneasily. "Come, baby, tell me. It doesn't matter. Nothing's so cruel that Charley wouldn't understand. You and Alice having money difficulties? I've got a lump saved …."

"Nothing like that Charley."

"Well, don't crucify yourself, my dear."

"You'll have to forgive me, honey. Will you?"

"Anything, baby."

"Well … er … er … I'm pregnant."

He dropped his gaze, then grinned at her. "Why are you to blame for that?" he asked. "Have the child. It won't be mine, but I'll love it anyway. You could have a dozen babies as far as I care. Your children will be my children, Frieta. Despite how you feel about it. Why, thousands of men marry women with kids every day. Not theirs, but they treat them better than their own fathers might have. Don't fret, my dear. You need me more so, now. And I need you. We can be married within a month. Go to Paris on our honeymoon. We can live again, Frieta. I love you. I love you!"

She bowed her head against his chest and sobbed in tears of bliss. It was done. She was saved. How could she judge whether Eddie's baby would not be the sweetest child on earth, or not?

Now that Charley and Frieta had vowed their love for each other, they put on wraps and he drove her back to the apartment. Alice still was not home. While Charley stood at the bedroom door, Frieta had suddenly became suspicious of Alice's intentions. She had vowed that she was going to kill Eddie.

Frieta actually knew that she kept the revolver in the bottom dresser drawer. So she hurried into her mother's bedroom and yanked the bottom drawer open. Charley came and watched her, the more suspenseful that something might have happened to Alice.

"What's th' matter, Frieta?" he asked. "What's happened?"

She fumbled under all the linens but did not find the revolver. Did Alice actually take the gun and go out to murder Eddie? A great dreadful suspensefulness hung over her.

She sprang to her feet. "Alice's revolver is missing," she said. "She boasted she'd kill Eddie for messing with me. It's his baby, Charley."

"Now don't get excited, darling," he said tenderly, taking her into his arms. "We'll call the police. They'll find Alice."

"Oh, God!" she cried. "I hope nothing's happened to her. Pray to God that it's not too late!"

CHAPTER THIRTEEN

FRIETA DID NOT HESITATE to phone Thomas McShane, who she found at his home on Waterway Drive. McShane informed her that he would be out to the apartment just as quick as he could locate Duke Wayne.

While Frieta waited for the detectives, she took a seat on the divan beside of Charley. She could find no words to speak her feelings, neither could he. They just cuddled and kissed between intervals, until they heard the police sirens outside.

Frieta opened the door for the cops. Wearing heavy black slickers, McShane and Wayne entered the apartment and Frieda closed the door.

"What's happened, Frieta?" McShane asked, speaking politely to Charley Boyles.

"It's Alice, McShane," Frieta said nervously. "She's taken the gun, and I assume she's out hunting for Eddie LaRose. She swore she was gonna kill him!"

"Why?" the cop asked.

"Because of me," she said shamefully. She dropped her head. Charley rose from the divan, moved over beside Frieta and steadied her. His presence seemed to add strength to her weakened constitution.

"What do you mean?" Duke asked.

"Eddie … oh, this is awful. Eddie … he … please. Don't question me so. Just find Alice."

"We have to know what's happening here, Frieta," said McShane. "If you don't tell us, how will we know who to look for and why?"

Charley kissed Frieta's fingers, pressing them hard against his full lips. She seemed to be encouraged enough to make the unchaste statement.

"I'm carrying Eddie's baby!" she confessed openly. "That's why Alice wants to murder him!"

Duke Wayne frowned. McShane studied Freita. Then both men obviously sensed the entire picture as it had been, as it had undoubtedly occurred.

"Thanks Frieta," McShane said to her. He gave her a consoling pat on the shoulder and turned quickly on his heels. "Come on, Duke. Let's go. We'll put out a quick flash to look for them. Eddie's hangout shouldn't be very hard to find. If they've left there, it's no telling." He went to the door. Duke Wayne followed him. McShane turned at the door and said, "Will you stay with her, Mr. Boyles?"

"Of course I will," Charley replied. "We're going to be married. Frieta and I are about to become engaged."

"Good," said Duke. "Congratulations." Then he followed McShane down the stairs.

Frieta was very upset by Alice's disappearance, and she did not have much desire to sleep. The rain did not let up, and she felt that it just might be a long vigil before the detectives returned or phoned of any results. She certainly did not want anything to happen to her mother, not after all which she had been through with Eddie LaRose. In a sense, she didn't care if Alice did kill the bum, whom she now loathed and despised. How foolish she had been not to have accepted Charley's proposal weeks ago. All her weeks of sufferings could have been sweet sensual moments of blissfulness.

By midnight when no word had come, Frieta pulled Charley into her bedroom. If anybody came she could easily get up and let them in. She did not have to coax Charley into imagining what she wanted. His intimate kisses had sparked the flame in her belly again. She was suddenly blind as to her troubles. Only her soul must be appeased.

In the bedroom, she removed her clothes. Naked, she flung herself upon the bed. Charley crawled into bed with her. Instantly her thighs tightened round his body. His contact made her give a wild sigh of sweetness. Then her body became a wild coiling creature which he could not halt. The more he took her, the more she gave and moaned and shimmied herself up to him with all the energies that her body possessed.

"I need you terribly ... so terribly bad."

"You're wonderful, Frieta. Oh, baby, you're worth a fortune in gold. Do it to me!"

His soft whispers intensified her wild energies. And while he teased her, telling her how good it felt and how she knew how to undulate her hips, and how the sensation pleased his soul, she responded with a freshness which he could hardly match.

When she felt the urgency of release about to happen, she flung her arms over her head and screeched so loudly in his face until she was ashamed of herself afterwards.

When they lay beside each other, smoking, in the dim glow of a table lamp, she looked into his loving eyes. Her voice was as primitive and lost as were her sexual desires.

"Do I make crazy things to you, Charley?"

"You're mad, baby," he grinned. "But, you know, I want you that way. Your passions are insatiable. Are you ready again?"

She looked at him, then felt along the lower part of his body. Indeed that sweetness on him was apt to respond again to her wishes.

"Charley, my God!" she groaned, throwing herself back upon her back and pulling him over her again. The contact pulsed her soul. She dimpled and clutched. She reeked with sweat, and twisted herself in all her remaining energy.

"Charley, please...please!" she begged. His own vitality increased, developed, grew in leaping bounds. She could not fight with his violent pace. "Charley...my heavens...you'll kill me... please...no...no...God...yes .. yes it's yes...it's....now.... now...Oh!" Her energies failed and she fell back exhausted and spent, much too sapped to make herself respond within the next few hours. The feeling was still with Charley, and she sensed it as he rose from the bed to go to the bathroom. She could only gasp at a man at his age who was always in such a condition. She knew, however, she would not have to worry about being unfaithful to a man of his respect. Charley was more animal when it came to sex, than human. But he was a sweet animal whom she was never going to let go.

When he returned to her, she looked to see how he felt again. The same potent responsiveness of his pestering device met her gaze.

Charley smiled at her, noticing her amazed expression.

He crawled into bed with her again. Instantly her hot breasts intensified him into virility. She felt him a fourth time, and a fifth, and a sixth during that first night. By morning she was unable to leave the bed. She couldn't have if she had wanted to. Her pregnancy had made her deathly sick again.

Charley was bathing Frieta's forehead when the knock sounded on the door. He left her and went to the front room. At half past six A.M., he did not imagine who it could be.

As he opened the door, in stepped Duke Wayne.

"Any news?" Charley asked.

"Nothing," Duke replied. "Where's Frieta?"

"In bed. She's having a sick spell. Her pregnancy, you know."

"I must have a word with her," Duke said.

Charley nodded and led the way into the girl's bedroom where they found her seated up in bed. Her questioning eyes studied Duke Wayne.

He held his felt hat. The rain had stopped, so he didn't wear a slicker. The sun was apt to shine.

"Well, any news of her?" Frieta asked before Duke could speak.

"Some, but not the people. At least we know she's with Eddie. The bartender at Cowboy Inn told us that they left there together around seven last evening. We've checked all hotels, no luck. We can't even locate that green car of Eddie's. That's why I'm here to see you, Frieta. Thought maybe you might give us a lead."

"What can I do?" she asked. "What can I say or tell you?"

"You stated yesterday that you and Eddie were intimate, somewhat. Just that he might have driven you some place during the course of your moments together?"

"Of course he did." she said.

"Any particular place away from town?"

"Yes. Once, I remember he drove me out on 32 Highway, and he parked the car along a gravel road just south of the highway and we talked."

"Do you remember the name of the road?"

"I didn't notice any name."

"Near the Kaw River?" he asked. "Was it near the Kaw River, Frieta?"

She nodded. "Yes, we have a nice view of the river. In fact, that was one of the main reasons why he drove out there, so we could watch the high river. Do you imagine he drove her out there?"

"It's a hunch," said Duke. "Thanks, Frieta. We'll shake out there. And see." He wheeled towards the door and they heard him slam the door and hurry down the stairs.

By eight A.M. Frieta's morning sickness had abated, and she motioned Charley into bed with her.

"I've got to have it," she whispered.

He removed his trousers and moved into bed beside of her. His lips went to her thrusting breasts. He suckled and teased her until she could not stand off his titillations any longer. Then she flung herself on her back and elevated her flanks.

"Take me. Take me, Charley. Please ... please, take me." He crawled over and took her madly. Afterwards, she fainted, but the sensation was to appease her soul's endless desire for him.

Alice was found. Thomas McShane phoned just before noon to make the announcement to Frieta and Charley. They had carried her on to the St. Margaret's hospital. She had a nasty wound in her right shoulder, had lost considerable blood and suffered from hysterical shock and exposure. Other than that she would recuperate. Alice had been conscious enough to tell them where Eddie was lying dead in the corn stalks. Eddie's body had been taken from the cornfield. The weapons had been recovered. A picture of Alice's half nude body and the wild scene around the car had been made. It was of little doubt that there had been a savage struggle before the fatal shot had killed Eddie LaRose.

Alice recuperated rapidly. In a few days she was able to leave the hospital. She was happy upon hearing that Frieta and Charley had gotten married a few days before she had left the hospital. Duke was a constant visitor. She felt that Duke and McShane might be able to get her off with a light sentence.

The trial was held three weeks later. McShane presented evidence which showed she had suffered rape, and attack, and finally tried to halt Eddie's mad desire to murder her. The fight in her apartment was brought into the arguments. Alice told how she had left the car to return back to town, and how Eddie had forced her back to the car, to finish ravishing her.

The trial lasted two days. When the jury returned with the not guilty announcement, Alice broke into tears.

Her killing of the hoodlum was in self defense. The entire courtroom was in her favor. She was appeased.

Duke Wayne accompanied Alice and Charley and Frieta back to the apartment after the trial. They had a fine dinner-party, somewhat of a celebration. Afterwards, Duke announced his intentions to marry Alice. She accepted him. And while Duke and Alice left the apartment to take in a fine motion picture, Frieta pulled Charley back into her bedroom and they went to bed.

Both naked, the bed whined and shook with their sexual delight. Frieta did not think she ever wanted to be cured of her morbid sex ailment, not as long as she had such a pleasuring device as Charley Boyles.

THE END

www.ingramcontent.com/pod-product-compliance
Lightning Source LLC
Chambersburg PA
CBHW030351180626
46812CB00007B/2849

9 7 8 1 9 5 4 8 4 0 1 2 6